# Exiting the Game

*Volume 1*

DONALD BEACH HOWARD JR.

authorHOUSE®

*AuthorHouse*™
*1663 Liberty Drive*
*Bloomington, IN 47403*
*www.authorhouse.com*
*Phone: 1 (800) 839-8640*

*Published by AuthorHouse   01/05/2016*

*ISBN: 978-1-5049-6674-0 (sc)*
*ISBN: 978-1-5049-6673-3 (hc)*
*ISBN: 978-1-5049-6675-7 (e)*

*Library of Congress Control Number:  2015920096*

*Print information available on the last page.*

*Any people depicted in stock imagery provided by Thinkstock are models, and such images are being used for illustrative purposes only. Certain stock imagery © Thinkstock.*

*This book is printed on acid-free paper.*

# A Positive Note

I Donald Beach Howard Jr., was born September 7, 1974 on Labor Day in a small town called Louisville Kentucky. I began writing this fiction novel called Exiting the Game, while being incarcerated at (CCA) in Nashville Tennessee in 2005. At this time, I was labeled as an inmate/drug dealer inside their life line program. I seen several individuals, who I knew were still living in Satan's dark world of pain and destruction. So I took it upon myself to focus my negative energy, and write a fiction novel which contained a lot of the street activities. Then turned it into a positive note for the world of life. I learn to listen, live right, and catch the naked eye with a creation of a gangster/drug dealer novel, which carries a true meaning to this world today. Because this novel was created to show others in the world, that anyone could change in a blink of an eye, if we just believe. Satan works in ways the inner spirit cannot understand, but with God by our side everything comes to the light.... Amen

## "Exiting The Game"

# *The New Beginning*

At the age of seventeen, I became a worker for Satan inside a small town called Louisville Kentucky. I was never to know that I was focused on a dream, which was never going to end. However, Satan showed a glass dream, that was soon to be shattered in a blink of an eye. I was dealt a handful of negative cards at a early age. I soon found out how to manipulate, lie, cheat, and steal. I could feel myself falling in the hands of a dark God with negative beliefs. Still I was a troubled kid at heart, with anger flowing throughout my veins. Never to know my father was murdered in the exact lifestyle by his own friend. I was lost on this dark journey fighting my own trials and tribulations here on earth. Therefore, fire racing throughout my veins ready to get paid in life. I was lead in a dark world of marijuana, cocaine, alcohol, and pills. Along with people who used and shot these drugs into their veins with needles. Basically torturing their own temple without any remorse. I felt Satan's dark vibes racing throughout my soul as well as ready to wheel and deal. Family members, mother, fathers, sisters, and brothers lusted for a narcotic I possessed in life. As I found out the hard way in life, because this would lead to my own karma on this negative journey. I was carefully schooled on how to create crack-cocaine. I would have divided these nuggets up into twenty-eight a gram, and have them ready to be severed like a fast food restaurant. This was a hot commodity and the price for this type candy was know where near cheap. Twenty-eight grams went for eight hundred to a thousand dollars a pop. This was a give and go business! Plus, a no friends game! If you came into this type of lifestyle as a boy, it definitely turned you into a man. I would always walk, talk, and keep my hand on the trigger at all times. Because in a blink of an eye anything could have gone down in this type of game. Robbed or Killed! I chose to killed or be killed in the cards I was dealt. However, three older cats were putting me down who I knew my whole life. The click was solid, and if you challenged anyone of us, it would be on like shoot it up bang-bang and everybody must die. This was the case in our eyes. Although, my stepfather let one female live, which was exception to the rule. This mistake gave him life without the eligibility for parole. I see all kinds of friends in my past life as a square Joe. Now they label me as the man with all the coke. I dwell in the projects like a small Nino Brown. If you weren't selling our narcotic on the block, you were asked to leave. If not! You were carried off one way or the other, peacefully, violently, of your own choice. I had three younger cats working under my supervision by the names of Wayne-Head, Shitty, and King-James. All three of them had hell racing from out their heart. They would kill their own mother and father if it needed to be, to show the loyalty. Of course, plenty females came with the game. They wanted to be involved with something much bigger in life. I was taught a female was like a viper, a snake, which could slip pass a male's security system without being peeped. Then we were in for the taking at any cost. Even if your life needed to be. So this is why I kept me two bad ass bitches on my side at all times. They were twins that most people couldn't tell them apart, but there was only one way! Angel had coal black silky hair and arched eyebrows, but Diamond had flat black hair and no arch in her eyebrows. They were two down to earth females, who knew how to treat me as a drug dealer. Both of them sat by my side watching every move I made like bulldogs. So when I was called for twenty-eight grams of half powder and half hard. I would respond by getting in touch with my three youngsters, and explain what the present buyer needed. One would stay by the vehicle running, while holding his firearm. It would be loaded, cocked, and ready to spoil a nonbeliever's intentions. However, the other two youngsters made the deal. One was the mouth piece to conduct business, while the other one like an eye spy on point. Watching every move, a person made in the house. He scooped out girlfriends, mothers, friends, even the kids. This was to make sure the transaction was successful without any bloodshed. After the deal was complete, I was called with it's a rap. Then the three youngsters would make their way to the honey-cone hideout to be safe. Therefore, the vehicle was switched. Then they would make their way to the presence of me, Angel and Diamond. The money was set aside, because I would ask questions about the transaction. This was to see if they felt safe or in a jam. A smile or a frown would let me know the business. However, a frown would piss me clean off, and time of business had to change. Then Angel and Diamond knew it was time to boot up. These two vipers would be set on a mission of let's get it without a doubt. I knew the game had to be played raw, because the negativity had to be plugged in a devilish way. The role I played was to get shit done in the right way. Even if it came down to misplacing a face from the game I played as a drug dealer. Then away two females went with Satan pulsing throughout their veins, ready to get close to a dirty soul. To put him or her to sleep in a nasty way without any remorse. For thinking negative thoughts or plotting against or table of life. I wasn't worried about the twins doing dirt, because my judgement day would come in due time. Still the twins stood there waiting on a response from me. Everything was a go at a hundred percent Wayne-Head explained. Then King-James blurted out! It was a smooth drop. The hood was like a ghost town, with bitches dropping it like it was hot ready to get a blast of the narcotic. After the fact a female was trying to sell her soul for a hit of the drug. Standing in their face shacking, begging, asking outlandish questions trying to get a free hit. Then he stated, that it hurt his feel with a sad look on his face. Quickly I cut the conversation short, and stopped him in his tracks. This is Satan's game homie! The strong survive and the weak must die. So what our youngster? Because I can feel there is loose love running in your heart, that needs to be fixed. He explained know that's not it Dee! So what is it then, and please answer with the right answer. Still Shitty, Wayne-Head, and the twins stood there waiting on an answer from their partner in crime. He quickly struck a conversation about his brother's situation. From letting me know of him being strung out on the narcotic. Deep down I could feel his pain, but that was the wrong feelings to contain as a drug dealer. So I pulled him by his collar, and told him in a nice way. That shit happens! Please deal with it because this drug has no friends. This drug takes over the mind, body and soul. My brothers in the same damn boat. If I let my pride and joy stand in the way. I'll fall weak in the dope game player. I learned to walk over my feelings and that shit hurts. Now my job is to serve the world, and protect this table of life at all cost. So snap out this fucked up state of mind, and let the world revolve. In this business a person needs a clear mind to be safe you feel me James? After the long conversation he nodded as if he heard me out and clear. So I continued to school him with knowledge, that was passed to me from Jam. I explain this shit to the table because I live by respect, honesty, and loyalty. However, this is to keep everyone safe in Satan's game. If one falls weak that could be the breaking of the camel's back, and this table will be destroyed. Does everyone understand? Everybody knew that I was talking from the heart, because my eyes were bloodshot red. So James spoke up out of the blue. I do understand Dee! I'll work on my inner feelings, that could cause a slight problem in our bondage as partners. What I need to focus on is this table of life, and just learn to get money. I could feel a good spirit lingering throughout my body like a blessing. So I quickly jumped up like a madman! Now let's get back to business, because Spider wants an ounce and a half out West. He has $1250 cash! Tell him to pay me the rest on the next re-up. Immediately the youngsters were in the wind to get the product from the honey cone hideout. When they arrived at the spot everything was ready to be delivered. The 42 g was placed on the scales, weighted, bagged, and secured safely inside the vehicle. Now the mission was in process to go make the transaction.

# CHAPTER 2

## *Time of Business*

The arrival of Spiders. James standing by the running Buick with the chrome 45 Colt P-10 waiting on a nonbeliever with the wrong intentions. However, Shitty trailed behind Wayne-Head, because he contained the narcotic for the buyer. Shitty approached Spider while Wayne-Head eyes on the prize. One older cat lingered in the living room, while the deal took place. Immediately after everything was set to make the transaction there was a knock at the door. It was unexpected visitor, and time of business had to change. So Shitty ask Spider to come to the vehicle to get the product? Spider got real upset about going outside to do the transaction. He felt vulnerable out in the open, and began calling him out of his name. So immediately I was called and it wasn't cool at all! Shitty explain the situation and what was going down, but not what he said. I was in flames and I ask to speak to Spider. I told him if that was me making the deal would he do it to me. There wouldn't be anyone in the house while I conducted business. It will be just you and me! No sisters, no brothers, no fucking body! Just us two! So do you trust me or not player? Yeah man it's cool he explained. Alright then my man! Please go to the car and make the deal, because I'm on a set schedule homie. You're slowing down my business, and I have shit to do now as we speak. Do u feel me man? Now let me speak to Shitty so we can get the ball rolling. Shitty get the 1,250 and give him the product from the vehicle. Your words are golden, so he's on your time. Plus, your word is the last words that needs to be said in any transaction. Our table is our table! What isn't from this table player I'll deal with it myself. So let's get it, and tell him about the money shit. That's all he needs to worry and about at this time! Then Shifty, Wayne-Head, and Spider went to the Buick that was still running. They were greeted by James. The deal was made, so the youngsters got in the vehicle and pulled off. Away they headed towards the honey-cone hideout to get off the polices radar. Then I was called again. Shitty said dealing with Spider was going to be a problem, because he wants to be a king. So I yelled out a king! A king of what? Then Shitty blurted out the streets. I could feel a hateful vibe dwell through my body which gave me the chills. No! I'm going to make a visit with Spider myself. So get here, and we'll talk from there youngster. After hanging up the phone, I wondered what to do with this nonbeliever that dwelled in the same game. When the youngsters arrived. I could see in their eyes there was something that they were afraid to tell me about the Spider situation. Wayne-Head started explaining how everything went down. How after getting the narcotic he called them do-boys, and that another word for flunky. I feel he needs to be touched in a way Dee, that a person cannot imagine. Because I'm not know ones do-boy! I could feel the devil lusting throughout three young hearts. Plus, everything that came from their mouth was directly from Satan Himself. Angel and Diamond standing waiting on a devilish call dressed in black, ready to judge a nonbeliever. I yelled out get my shit! Angel quickly left my side, and went towards the room to get my problem solver. She brought me a change of clothes, that would blend in with the shadows so I wouldn't be seen on the block. I knew I had to be invisible, so I got dressed and put on the Teflon vest. Then grabbed my 9mm Kiel Tex with the built on infrared beam and scope. I told them nobody gets away when it goes down when this baby is in my hand. When everything hit's the fan please don't nut up. Because no nut, no glory! So let's do this quick, fast, and in a hurry. Make no mistakes! I have to get home to my wife and kids before this shit hit's the news. Quickly we all loaded up into the vehicle with a sense of hell, and were out to do the work of Satan Himself. Minutes away from our destination, I was called for two ounces. One soft and the other hard. I started thinking to myself, should I get this money or the nonbeliever. I couldn't decide so that's when Satan stepped in and made the final decision. Therefore, in a way I couldn't remember so I wouldn't nut up. We were all headed towards the forbidden spot where life, and death both existed at the same time. As we pulled up to the area it appeared to look like a ghost town. I felt as if I was being peeped out, but there was no one in the area. With my heat seeker on my hip, I quickly rushed into the building where everything was supposed to go down. As I walked off the elevator onto the second floor there were two females standing in front of Spiders door getting ready to knock. So I cleared my throat to get their attention. Can I help you ladies with something? They both turned and smiled with a spaced out look on their faces. I ask why they were there? I could see in their eyes that they were already wired up and wanted to be re-up on this of drug. Spider was expecting them so he could pull a trick with them both at the same time. The girls were two friends who had no money, but wanted to sell their bodies for the next hit. I felt as if I was just in the nick of time for the taking, while his guard were down. Spider thinking to see two spaced out bitches ready to be freaked. So I thought the scene out. The takeover was going down with two spaced out hoes. Who happen to be at the wrong place at the wrong time, and six angry spirits out for blood. Still ready to let loose and bring judgment down on him and the click. The girls locked on the door repeatedly. I could hear footsteps growing closer to the door so I backed up to be safe. Then I heard a male voice from the other side of the door yelling out, there here boss out of excitement. Spider said ok and open the damn door! Suddenly, the door swung open and we came in like hell was to freeze over. We started handling our business! One dude yelled out it's a set! Gun shots rang out and the room lit up like 4th of July. That's when two of Spiders partners, and the two chicks were killed immediately during all the gun fire action. I pointed my gun directly at his dome, at point blank range. Then told him to hurry up and put some clothes on, because we were going for little ride. As he started getting dressed, out of fear he asked was he going to die? To let him know I meant business. I told him that if he made any sudden moves, he would be left here to rot like his friends on the floor. So stop staling, asking questions, and come on! Look here buddy! You already know what the deal is Spider? It's your damn mouth! I don't like how you disrespect this table of life. You know I have a reputation and business to maintain. Now you sit here crying out for a soldier to spare your ass. Oh yeah! By the way! There's someone who wants to talk to you personally in seventeen different ways. If you know what I mean! We all head back down to the vehicle, and dipped out from the negative area. To get to the lowest spot, like the book of dominos.

# CHAPTER 3

## *Time of Judgement*

As we arrived at the spot, his blind fold was removed. Out of fear he screamed for his life. No the country! I don't owe you any explanation or excuse. Talk to them! The three youngsters blurted out, I'm no errand-boy or flunky. So go ahead and talk the same way you did earlier, but act like Dee isn't around. This way I can judge you in several different ways sucker. You see my team still stands, and you're the only one left from your table. Them boys died because of a negative friend like you, and you supposed to be a true leader. So do have anything else to say for yourself Spider? Yes! I know yawl pissed and I understand. Man I got kids to feed and I want to live. Yeah I do understand the kid situation, but you choose your own way out in life. I'll send a check for life monthly! I really will miss you Spider! We all will! Then I turn and look at the three youngsters, Angel and Diamond. As I walked away I yelled out in a devilish voice, that shit happens. Wayne-Head stepped up, and I could see in Spiders face that it was going to be his last words. With tears of death in Spiders eyes, seventeen shots rang out in a row. This put an end to his fears and any sorrow he may have felt, but it was too late. His time was up! Spider laying in a pool of blood, body shacking, because of the nerves which lingered throughout his body. As he slowly drifted off into an everlasting coma I felt good about myself. He was then put into a body bag, carried off, and placed in the back of Peewee's trunk. Peewee took his body away to be misplace and to never be seen again. I asked Wayne-Head how he felt? We got one down, and many more to go! Especially, if we still playing the game as drug dealers. We gave DAP on that, as I laughed. While Angel and Diamond escorted me to my vehicle that I had parked over Peewees. I started explaining to Shitty, James, and Wayne-Head, that this is a done deal. I have to get home to my wife and kids before someone finds out what just happened. Tomorrows a new day, and I'll holler back at yawl later. I returned home, and I was greeted at the door by my wife, and the two youngest kids Trey and Toni. Randy explained that she was looking at the news, and there was a shooting out West. A black Buick was spotted leaving the scene in a hurry with two females and a male who could be a suspects. The male was seen wearing black and blue army fatigues. She asked if I knew about the gun play that went down early this afternoon? No and why! Randy it's your job to take care of the family situation and nothing else. While I was talking to my wife Trey and Toni ran to give me a big hug, because they were happy to see daddy. I explained to them both I just entered the house and I was tired. I need a shower, with a little shut eye. I let them both down, while making my way towards the bathroom. I got in the shower wondering to myself who the eye spy, and did he or she get a close look at me. Standing in the shower I place my hands on the wall, while the hot water ran down my back. Still hoping the water would wash my sins down the drain with it. As I continued to zone out. I felt my wife place her soft hands on my back as she entered the shower with me naked. She asked me what happen because she knew I was lying through my teeth? Again I explained nothing in an angry voice! Baby can you please end this conversation? While turning around looking into her dark brown eyes, and she could feel the dark presence that lingered in the bathroom. I'm sorry! Baby shit happens for a reason, especially when a man crosses the line out of disrespect. Someone negative has to pay their dues in this dirty game. Understand me in the right way sweetie! Slowly I got out the shower, and stood in front of the mirror shacking the water off my face. After bending over holding onto the sink thinking about who the eye spy really was. Randy began explaining in a soft voice, whatever happen in streets, leave it in the streets. Baby you can't think about the past, and now you must continue to move forward for the sake of our family. She grabbed my hand from the shower and gave me a kiss. I looked into her dark brown eyes, and I could feel that side of myself lost. I turned and walked into my bedroom blurting out I love you sweetie. I felt were my wife was coming from, because she didn't want to lose me to the street life. When I entered the bedroom, I was greeted with burning candles, food on the hot plate, and a bottle of Don P. I could feel a loveable presence lingering through the bedroom, like all my sin were being erased or forgotten. When she entered the room, she asked if I like the special candle light dinner. I just smiled with a feeling of overwhelming happiness in my heart, and asked her why? Love will make a wife do anything in life if the chemistry and bondage is there baby. I just smiled again, because I was at home. Home Sweet Home! Thank you for your time and patience Randy! This is the reason why you carry my last name Miss Bishop! I could feel a slight presence of love lusting in the air. It felt like it was a spiritual awakening lingering in an out the bedroom without any worries at all. Then I slowly sat on the edge of the bed, as she handed me the plate. As she popped the cork from the bottle, I gazed into Randy's eye having freaky thoughts. While she poured my Don P into the glass the hormones got stronger. Still it was time to give the Lord his thanks for this blessed dinner. Then I started to eat the meal she prepared. While she stood there gazing at me taking every bite, she asked if it was good? Baby how does it taste with a slight grin on her face? I just smiled, while taking a sip of the Don P. After eating the candle light dinner, I was full as hell. I was relaxed, and ready to get a little shut eye. So I thanked her for the dinner, and told her the bed is calling my name. Therefore, I quickly went in the bathroom and wash my hands, so I can race back to the bed. Once I crawled into the bed, I was out like a light. The next morning, I was awakened at 6:15am by the early smells of bacon, eggs, sausages, pancakes, and a cup of milk. My wife explained Shifty, James, and Wayne-Head were in the living room waiting on me. They were waiting on the first call of the day, so we could get the ball rolling.

# CHAPTER 4

## *Home sweet Home*

I could feel that this morning was special, and the day was just beginning. I was called for two ounces of all RAW powder. I told the three youngsters to go to the spot. Bag up the 56 grams, and take it to Silk, who stayed on the North side of town. He has 1,650 and it is all good. They quickly went to the vehicle to make their way towards the honey-cone hideout to get the product. They arrived at the spot, grabbed the cocaine, and bagged the 56 grams. Away they went to make the transaction with Silk out North. When the youngster reached their destination I was called. I explained everything was still ago, and he is waiting on yawl. As they pulled up to the area, he was standing outside with three females calm as hell. Silk slowly stepped away from them the females to approach the vehicle with money in hand. Shitty was sitting on the back seat asking him to get in, so they could get down to business. He opened the door and climbed in to greet the youngsters. Shitty and Silk did the exchange of the drug and money. He explained to the youngsters that this is a dirty game. So they need to stay safe, and stick to the rules on the table. Only the strong survive in this game. Then open the door and got out. He started walking back into the mist of the three female. Then he yelled out, remember what I said youngsters. As they pulled off to get out of the negative area they remembered it was the same thing I had said. Shitty gave me a call and said it was a Rap, while blurting out Silk seems to be a cool cat. He's cool I explain, but it's a long story. He is one my old friends, who lingered on another table with me when I was young. Before all the shit hit the fan! It was five of us on the table of life. Jam, De' Shot, Silk, Dre, and Me! Jam ran the show! Me and De' Shot was the only two who could get close to him. Me and Dre were the transporters and made shit happen. Silk and Dre took care of everything that got in the way or whoever fell weak at the table. Then one day we got ratted out by one that was from our own table. The police was tipped off where we would be getting the drugs together, and they rammed through the door like a hot sunny day. De 'Shot and Turtle reached for their straps, and were hit six times in the chest, one in the neck. They both died instantly! Silk was shot one time in the arm. Jam was sitting at the table with nowhere to go, but down with the ship. Then when me and Dre arrived, it looks like a SWAT meet that was in for the taking. I could feel that Dre had something sneaky lingered through his soul. He said to me that we were the only ones left from the table of life. It was more in the streets for thee both of us now. To me it felt like God and Satan were getting ready to go to war. So I asked where was the respect that revolved around Jams table? Fuck Jam, he responded! I got out the vehicle with hell racing through my veins, because I wanted to do my own partner-in -crime in now. Still it wasn't the right time, plus I found the weak link of our table. I know he would be dealt with in due time, so I made my way home. I sat waiting on a letter or a phone call from Jam. So I could let him know of what went down at the spot. Three days came to pass, and it was their funeral. It was one of the saddest days of my life. I was standing next to both of their mothers, while hearing other spirits crying out to the Lord in pain. Looking at them close their casket and lowering them to the resting place hurt like hell. I felt the fire running through my flesh, but it was nothing I could do at this time. However, I will be there to see you Dre in due time it began lingering in my mind over and over again. So I had to leave the funeral before I really did explode. Getting into my vehicle I seen De' Shots mother leaning against her car in pain because she just lost her only son. I knew I had to cheer her up because we were like brothers. So I ask her how do you deal with a problem mama? She explained in little words, that the problem stands there, because you allow it to be in your way. She was right! Dre must die was ringing in my mind. I thanked her for the conversation, and gave her hug to show the love. So I got in the car, and went home to my family. When I walked into the house, I could feel the loveable spirits rumbling throughout the house. All eleven children sitting at the table as one big happy family. Everyone eating their daily meal with nothing to worry about shinning in their faces. I heard Randy asking who was that coming in the door? Trey and Ja'Cori screamed out daddy is home! She came from out the kitchen with love all over her body. She asked if I was ready to eat lunch? Your plate is in the microwave baby! I knew I had to hide the pain about Dre. I explained to my wife about how nice the funeral was, and who came to give their respects to both families. She could see straight through me! She could feel my pain but someone had to stay strong. Again she asked if I was ready to eat? Yes, cupcake I'm ready to eat. Then I turn and walked in to my bedroom to get a peace of mind. I sat on the edge of the bed wondering in space. I thought about how tight our table was in the card we were dealt. I kept thinking what Jam would do in this type of situation. I knew he wouldn't give up in life. Suddenly I could hear my wife calling my name, but I couldn't move. It felt like my body was paralyze. My mind was focus on the game and what needed to be done. When she stumbled into the room, with the plate of food in her hand. One for me and the other for herself I felt special. Then she wanted to know what I wanted to drink with my lunch. I couldn't even speak at this time, because my body was full of emotions. My mind was focus on the snitch needed to be dealt with at a hundred percent. Dre was still breathing in the streets and he had to be stop now. So my wife Struck up a family conversation to clear my mind from the street life. She knew I was full of painful thoughts, but something had to change. Baby what about a cook out with the family my wife asked? So let's grill today? Yeah! Let do hamburgers, hotdogs, steak, and pork chops. While talking I could still feel the hate running through me. So I walked outside to check on my two Pitts. I asked her if the kids feed the dogs? Yes, and calm down, because you are making me nervous. I felt she was right, and the kids didn't need to see me like this. I was walking in the footsteps of Satan Himself. In a state of mind that I dwelled in, which felt like hell on earth. I unchained both dogs to let them run around the backyard. They look as if they were free, and wanted to say fuck the world. So I called their names, Woo and Muff Quickly they came running toward me, like holy spirits lingering through their bodies. Their eyes were full of happiness and excitement with seeing the master of the house. The one who keeps them clean, full, and plenty of exercise, so they could stay in shape. I commanded them to sit! They immediately obeyed me and took a seat. I was hurting in the inside because I could feel the love. I could see the respect that was lingering in both dogs. My wife explained to me that everyone isn't free. Baby every dog has it day in due time, because it will come to the light. So come help me focus on what linger here at this table at home. Me and these damn bad ass kids then smiled. I asked her to get the grill started, and what's cooking chicken? Minutes later, I could hear Toni and Ja'Cori growing closer towards the backyard. When they got to me, I was play with the dogs. Thinking how to get close to Dre, and put the Smack Down on a nonbeliever. I explained to my wife, I had to make a quick run. So I made my way to the family vehicle, and went on a tour around town. I was focus on the streets, but planning how the shit needed to go down. I pulled up into Mc Donald's to get a bite to eat. A female was working on her vehicle. She was trying to change her tire. So I walked over and gave her a hand. She knew me through her sister. Her sisters name was Angel. I had to take repeat, because they look dead alike. Yeah! I know Angel but I didn't know she had a twin. She explained that her and Angel were twin, but she was out of town at the time. She was coming back in town tomorrow night. After placing the tire on, I gave Diamond my phone number to give to Angel. I need her to do something for an old friend that needs a helping hand. The tire was placed on and she thanked me for helping her out. Because I wouldn't have gotten the tire on right. I just smiled, but I need you to get the message to your sister and that will be enough. I turned and made my way into the restaurant for a bite to eat, and I was greeted by Dre himself. He responds with long time no see player! I could feel a bad present, and he had something planned for me. Then three cats approached by his side with a negative vibe that gave me the chills. He started explaining these two cats lingered on his new table of life. This is Hubba 10 and Reese! I could feel the hell lingering throughout their flesh. They kept their eye on the prize, like I was a Big Mac special. I felt kind of shuck up with my guards down. I told him that business on my side was hard, and I might need a helping hand to get back up. He just smiled in a devilish way and said ok. After turning around, he explained for me to give him a call when I was ready. I knew then I was in for the taking if everything was played right. Because this was my only chance to nip the snitch in the butt. I ordered my food, and ate my meal thinking of my next move. Therefore, after eating my meal, I made my way back towards the house.

# CHAPTER 5

# *The Family Get Together*

When I arrived back home, I made my way inside the house. I could smell fried pork-chops, greens, and jiffy cornbread cooking in the kitchen. I knew I was home at last! My wife walked up to me, and gave me a special kiss. She began asking me, if my mind was clear of what lingered on it earlier today? Baby I'm cool! I just needed to get a little fresh air and relax. But in the back of my mind, I knew everything was piecing itself together like a puzzle. So I looked at her and smiled! I gave her a kiss on the chick, and walked towards our bedroom. I stood in the room in a daze, looking at both my homeboy's obituary. Then suddenly my cell phone began to ring. It was Angel! She was glad to hear from me, because it's been six years or more since we spoke to one another. I told her that I got married, and had eleven kids to feed. She asked who the luck lady was? I explained Randy from Fern Creek High School! She was the Square Jo in your math class! You and her had gym 3$^{rd}$ period together do you remember? Yeah, because she was short, brown skin, thick, with haze brown eyes. That's her Angel! Plus, I got some big business going down in a couple days, and I need you on this one sweetie. This mission is to put an unhappy frown on this old friend's face. Do you feel me Angel? I do understand so let's get it partner. So set up the sting, and I'll do the rest player! I sat on the phone in a daze, because she was the same game Pitt that never changed in years. So I told her if you needed anything just call, and it would be a done deal. I'm depending on you sweetie! Call me in the morning, so we can get the ball rolling. After talking to Angel, I went into the living room to chat with my wife. We began talking about the family situation. Then I asked her if she wanted to go out tomorrow night? She just looked into my eyes, because she knew something was going down slick. So she asks if there was anything that she should be informed about, with a devilish look on her face. It felt like she was reading me like a book without the cover, and my expressions was giving me away. Yes, or No she explained? Yeah! You know I'll be there with yawl, but I just have to make a short run somewhere baby. I'll be back in a blink of an eye, because I have to take care of a little business. Baby I promise you daddy we be back soon. Plus, I will have something very special for you as soon as I return. She slowly turned around and walked into the kitchen to pat out some more hamburgers for the grill. I knew she was upset, but shit had to be done this way. I could feel the pain which lingered in my wife's temple, because she knew Satan was winning in my lifestyle I chose as a drug dealer. When she came from out the kitchen with several patted out hamburgers ready to hit the grill, a family member pulled up. It was Rodney! He was a Square Jo, but cool as hell. When we greeted him, he asked if I changed my lifestyle? I just looked at him with a slight grin, and let his ass have it in nice words. Is this a question you should be asking me in front of my wife? I thought this was a blessed day for the family, because all the food smells good right? So does anyone want a beer? No thank you Rodney said! So what would you like to drink? Fuck the drink Dee! Then he got to explaining about his job, and he needed some help in two weeks on a construction project. I told him if I wasn't tied up, I would be glad to help a hard working family member. I called both my dogs to tie them up, because I didn't want anyone to get bite on a humble. After tying my dogs up, I walking into the house to find my wife. She was standing in the hallway with her hands on her hips. I told her that I needed to be a preacher, because her cousin talked to much for me. Then I could hear other family members entering the house hollering out Randy name. It was the Bread winning Capri! I knew she had some weed to calm down my way of thinking. My wife went to greet her, because they were thick as thieves. I knew today was just the beginning, and I walked into the kitchen to season the steak for the grill. While seasoning the steaks my phone began to ring! It was programmed for a distinct ring for Dre! So I walked into my bedroom to get the phone, but it missed his call. So I called him back to see what the business was all about! He asked if I was ready to get down to business. I told him I had family over and I was tied up at the moment. So he understood were I was coming from, so I told him I would call him in my free time then hung up the phone. After hanging the phone, I started feeling that angry vibe crawling up my chest. However, I knew I had to keep a happy expression on my face to bypass my wife's security system. So I went to ask my wife if she wanted to take a ride with me to rent a new DVD movie from Blockbuster? She just smiled and blurted out, you must be reading my mind sweetie. I could tell she was starting to relax a little more, while the family member was around. Still the pain in my heart, I knew it had to be covered up for my family's sake. Therefore, I went to get in the car, while she explained to the kids we were going to get a movie or two. Backing out the driveway, I thought how it was to go down with the Dre situation. So away we went towards Blockbuster! On the way to the video store my phone began to ring. It was Angel! She was back in town, because she caught an early flight home. I told my wife, to go get the movies, that everyone would like to see. I just needed some time to talk important business on the phone with my partner. Plus, I been waiting on this call from hell! She gave me a kiss, and made her way inside the video store to purchase the movies. Angel told me that the plane just landed in the Ville, and she couldn't get in touch with Diamond to get a ride home. So I told her me and Randy would be there soon, if it's cool with her sweetie. So I got out the car and went into the video store to inform my wife of the situation. After telling her the business she said fine, but remember we do have family members at the house. That would be a bad example to show them, if we are gone for a long time Dee. I could tell deep within my wife flesh, she didn't want to do it but it was getting ready to be crunch time the city. I could feel the heat dwelling inside her flesh, but she never knew Angel was in town for me. So away we went towards the airport to get Angel. But my wife sitting there like she was ready to turn a beautiful day into a fucked up nightmare. Therefore, I started explaining the real reason why Angel was in town. I could see what lusted in her heart was slowly fading away. Then she blurted out, you should just explain the situation to me in a disappointed voice. Randy something, I need to keep things to myself cupcake, because you're my wife for one. Two I try to keep you and the kids safe out of harm's way. Third, is I'm living in a dark world of destruction, and the strong must survive in this game I play as a drug dealer. One slip can send me to prison or the grave yard. Do you understand me love? Believe me, I'm not trying to keep anything from you. I just want to keep all the negative shit in the streets where it belongs. This is the only way I know how to live. But if something were to go wrong, I know you and the kids would be straight. My job is to make sure you have everything in life, and don't need for nothing while I breath here on earth. So as a long as I have breath in my body this family of mine will be great. I could see the joyful tears in her eyes, because she understood everything I was saying without a doubt. Pulling into the airport, I knew it was going to be hard to find Angel because people were everywhere.

Thinking to find Angel, she found us first. So we got out the vehicle to get my new partner in crime. Angel and my wife began to talk, while I grabbed her luggage to place it in the trunk. After everything was loaded we got in the car and made our way towards Diamonds spot. On the way to her house, they got to talking about high school. Especially, when I had a jerry-curl while running track. Angel explain that her sister stayed out South in the projects. So I hit the interstate, so we would get there in five tops. After pulling up at the crib, I asked her if she was straight? Yeah she explained, while telling me that she had a house key to her apartment. So I quickly grabbed the luggage from the trunk, and carried it into her apartment. I told her to call me in the morning, because I have family shit going down at the house as we speak. So when you call I'll explain the business, and who needs to be dealt with sweetie. Then first thing tomorrow I have a little family shit to do, and after that we can get down to business. However, I have to go now! Because I can't leave my wife in the car to long, because this is a negative area with my guard's down. Just call me in the morning, and thank you for coming like you said you would Angel. As I started walking out the door, she whispered seductively, Randy was a very lucky girl and smiled. I just laughed, while continuing to walk towards the car feeling the true love in the air. When I got into the car, my wife was sitting with her arms cross ready to go home to the family. So away we went back to the house to spend family time. Home at last! I could see the kids running around like wild animals. I was upset in a way, but happy to see my plan slowly coming together. When I walked inside the house, I felt loveable spirits everywhere. As I smelled the aroma from the food, which made me hungry as hell. The I walked into the kitchen to see what was done cooking. The soul food was stacked high on plates neatly. Then I heard Rodney and Capri, laughing real loud in the backyard. So me and my wife went to see what was so funny, and let them know we were back from Blockbusters. I could see they were both high as hell, because Capri's eye was bloodshot red. I asked them both a question, and they laughed like I was a clown in a funny suit. Then I asked if they save us a blunt? Capri just reached in her pocket, and pulled out a fat sack of white rhino. I knew this type of hydro was the shit, and my type of freak medicine. I knew was time to get high, because my mind was still set on what needed to happen tomorrow night. While Randy rolled up this good smelling puff stick, I thought to myself how everything was to take place with the Dre situation. Because in my book, a snitch must die! After she lit up the famous puff stick, I knew the angry inside was going to go up in a puff of smoke. It was going to focus my mind on something else in seconds. When she passed it to me, I inhaled the bright white smoke for three to four seconds tops. I felt the THC creeping down my lungs, and my eyes were slowly closing. Everything I was mad about was quickly lost in smoke. The weed made me feel relaxed and calm. I stood there looking at my wife with a freaky look from hell, because she already knew what time it was now. Randy grabbed my hand, while explaining to the family they could help themselves to the food and drinks. My wife and I turned to walk inside the house to get the party started right. While walking into the house Randy whispered nasty, sexy, loveable things in my ear to keep my full divided attention. Capri blurted out you damn freaks and laughed out loud! Randy just turned around and said, just having baby making days with my husband. Rodney and Capri burst out laughing, while we walked inside the house. I went and set on the edge of the bed to get relax. Then Randy came and stood in front of me, while bending down with a smirk on her face. I guess it was to see if I was ready to bring another baby into this world. So I answered the question for myself! It's up to you cupcake, while laying back on the bed with my arms cross behind my head. As I kicked off my shoes, I knew it was going down tonight at a hundred percent. She climbed on top of me, caressing my clean shaved face. Then started rubbing my jaw muscles in a circular motion. Minutes later, she began taking off my clothes to get the party started. Randy licked my chest up and down as if I was a lollypop. I knew it was going down like New Years! I could feel her heart beating through my chest. As I made my way on top, I could feel the chemistry coming into play. I felt it was more in life than being a drug dealer. I knew she was my soul mate, and God placed her in my life for a reason. I was beginning to realize something different, but I still had to play my cards right to keep my family safe. I felt she deserved more in life! Then there was a knock on the door, and we had to stop. I quickly jumped up, and grabbed my robe to see who was at the door. It was Alicia and Zoe! With a lot on my mind Alicia began telling me about her bad day. Zoe just leaning against the wall with his eyes half way shut. I could see he had a long day with his daughter, but I was glad to see my children happy know matter the cost. So I quickly end the conversation by explaining, that I had to be their daddy every step of the way. But I love yawl both and I need some sleep. So if yawl need me for anything knock on the door, and I will be there at all times of the day or night. Then I shut the door behind them, and looked at my wife. I could see that she was happy, because I took a time out to be a true father. Then crawled back into the bed to comfort my wife, while asking her how does it feel to be free? In a sad voice she responded. We all have sinned here on earth, and some has fallen short from God's grace baby. Everyone has a chance to make a change and grow up. We just have to choose what lifestyle we want to live. If we make the wrong choice, I believe the Lord will allow us to correct it and make it right. Then she moved closer to me, and laid her head on my chest. She let me know that she had true love in her heart for me and family. So I sat there thinking to myself, why was I living the lifestyle as a drug dealer. I knew she was tired and out of energy, so I just laid still until she fell asleep. While she was asleep, I focused my mind on the Dre situation because this shit had to be done no matter what. Still hoping and praying that everyone would be safe when the shit hits the fan. Gazing at the ceiling in deep thought, I could feel my eyes slowly closing, and I was out like light.

# CHAPTER 6

## *Today Is the Day*

The next morning, I woke up by the sound of Thomas and Trey arguing about a damn video game. I made my way into their bedroom, and asked what was the problem? They responded with we can't get along, because one was cheating on the game. I could feel Satan's vibe running through their room. I didn't respond in the wrong way! I just took the game, and turned to walk away. I went back into my bedroom. And fell into a deep thought. When I zoned out like I wasn't even there! A part of me was like, I was having a deep conversation with Satan about the Dre situation. Randy came from out the bathroom brushing her teeth smiling, getting ready to get the ball rolling for tonight. I asked her if she wanted to stop at Shoney's to get a bite to eat? She replied, before going to the game room. Yeah! So Shoney's it was! She stated that we still needed to stop at the bank to get some more cash. I nodded my head and walked away to tell the kids to get ready. Then my phone began to ring! Trey came running around the corner with my phone in his hand. It was Dre! He was telling me that the deal was going down at Denise's house out East around 6:30pm sharp. I looked at my watch, and it was already 2:45pm. I didn't have a lot of time left to get the remaining of my plan together. So I told him that was cool with me! I would be there on time! I remembered that I had one last quick stop to make. Knowing in my mind the deal was set, and ready to go down at a hundred percent. I had to call Angel! Sounding a little nervous, she told me I've been waiting on your call. I need to know the last minute plan on tonight? I asked her did she have any protection? She started laughing! So I guess that meant yes! Meet me at the game room in about an hour. I'll be in the snack room getting a bite to eat. Angel don't be late! Everything revolves around our perfect timing. One mistake and both of us could get the bad end of the stick. I need you to be quick, like a fox hunting down its prey. Do you understand where I'm coming from? Yes, I understand! You want me to move like the wind, and be out like magic. That's right my girl! I'll meet you there shortly. I need to get my family out the door, so I will be on time. Then we both hung up the phone! I continued to talk to my wife about the change of plans. I couldn't stop at Shoney's because I would be late for Dre. Then I asked if the kids were ready to go have fun, and we needed to drive both vehicles. Let the girls would ride with you and the boys with me. So we both agreed! At the same time, I could feel my wife wasn't comfortable about us taking two cars on this family trip. I called Ja'Cori! I told him to gather the boys, and meet me at the car. He ran off screaming lets go, and the boys are riding with daddy. As we were loading up to leave, Rodney pulled up with his daughter. He was talking to me about his baby mother situation. She drove here from Tennessee, and wanted him to spend time with his daughter while she clubs it. I felt he still had his heart open to her, but things just weren't going to work out. The situation gave me the chills and pissed me off at the same damn time. I asked him if they wanted to tag along with us, and the family gathering is on me. Rana just smiled! I knew he didn't won't to be seen with me in public, because of the lifestyle I was living. I told him this was just a time out for the family. No business taking place, so you and Rana would be safe. Time was ticking! I had Rana to ride with all the girls.

After she got into the car, my wife drove on towards the bank to get some extra cash. We went on to the game room! My boys had such joy on their faces, because for once the whole family was going to spend the day together. I talked to my son's on the way. I wanted them to know the rules once we arrived. One mess up, and everybody will go back home. I had planned to stay for an hour or two, so that I could watch my family enjoy themselves. I didn't want to hear any excuse from anyone when we hit the game room. Not even my wife! Do we all understand? I could hear all four of them blurt out ok. I knew in my heart that when I left my wife was going to let them run wild. I told Rodney I had to leave the game room for about an hour, but I would be back. I have some important business to take care of today. Can you stay with your cousin until I return? He nodded his head, but making a fucked up comment! You need to make it quick, because these are your kids. I knew he would be ok, so I gave him a hundred-dollar bill. Because he wouldn't have to wait on my wife. As we pulled into the game room parking lot, I could feel time was growing near. It was almost time to say my goodbyes to an old friend who turned his back on the table. As we got out of the vehicle making our way towards the entrance. I could see from a far off distance, this sexy female pulling up to park. It was Angel! She just smiled because I haven't seen her in six years. I told you I wouldn't be late! I told her that I couldn't believe she was on time like clockwork. We can talk in the food court! Rodney was standing there with a grin on his face a mile long asking me who is the queen? I told him her name was Angel. He immediately wanted me to hook them up. I told him I would try, but she wasn't really into looking for a relationship at the time. I let him know she was my business partner, but he didn't give a damn. I didn't want to mix business with pleasure because it could lead to a problem. So we finally made our way inside the game room so the kid could have fun. In my mind I could only think about me having to get rid of a snitch dealer, that once was like my own brother. I had to make peace with my home-boy De' Shot and Turtle. I quickly met with Angel in the food curt! She was standing in line ordering her something to eat. I asked her if she was ready to handle the business? Dee I'm always ready to get down to business! Everything is set to go down tonight. I'll meet Dre out East over Denise's house. When I climb into the car, I need you to open fire and let him have it. Baby with all you got! I need Dre out the picture. I'll feel better about all the past shit once he is handled. He became a snitch and left my home-boys to die. I felt the pain throughout my body, but every dog has their day eventually. This night was finally coming to an end. Then I heard my wife's voice! As Angel waited on my signal I went to greet my wife. She was happy I was waiting on her to arrive. Angel and my wife started to have a friendly conversation, while I kept my eyes on the clock. I couldn't afford to let this opportunity get away from me. I had a long talk with my wife about the kids running around wild. Of letting her know how I wanted the boys to act, and they better not start any trouble. I felt a lot of fear in my wife's voice while talking to her about my lifestyle. I explained to her I was running short on time, and Dre was waiting on me. So I had to move quick baby! Randy stood there with tears pouring down her face, because she didn't know if I was going to return in one piece. I wiped the tears from her eyes, and reassured her that everything was going to be ok. In mind I wasn't really sure about the things that was going to take place. I gave her a kiss on her lips and said goodbye! I turned and looked at Angel, asking her if she was ready to get started. She stood up and walked toward the exit door of the game room. I let Angel know that everything was going to be fine. I told Rodney that our children didn't need to see the disappointed look on my wife's face. Once again I kiss her on her chick, and I walked out the exit door. I sat in the car in a deep thought hoping things would be played out just right. I started my vehicle and drove off. Angel trailing behind me like an undercover officer. I felt Satan talking to me in the back of my mind. He was letting me know, that there was no turning back now. As we grew closer to the spot, I was going over last minute details. This was to make sure our tracks would be covered. I called Angel on her cell phone to let her know where to park the car. When I pulled in front of Denise's house, it was like a block party. With drug dealers standing everywhere waiting on Dre. He came from out the house with a smile on his face saying, I've been waiting on you Dee. So now we can get down to business. I started thinking again how this plan was going to take place. It looks like a block party, so I was going to leave everything up to Angel. I still could feel that the area was getting ready to be a grave site for a couple of his homeboys. My heart was still set out to do this for my friends know matter what. I promise my home-boy's this would be Dre's judgment day. So I needed to get back in rhyme. He reached over and pulled out two kilos of cocaine from out the trash can. I stood there with fire rushing from out my head ready to explode. I told him that anything would work on my come up. Then he pulled out some triple beam scales, and weighted 252 grams of cocaine. He handed me nine ounces of all brick powder, and asked if that was enough? I just nodded my head yeah, and what's the ticket for the product. 5,600 for the product and smiled. I kept the pain bottled up inside, because I knew today was the day for everything to come to an end. I was hoping this problem would be dealt with in a positive way, and Angel making it out safe. I told him I had to pick up my family before it got too late. We started back to the front of the house, so that I could get in my car. I stood in front of the car talking to him about the business that was going down. He told me to be safe, and that the area was hot like a fire cracker. I got in the vehicle, rolled down the window to give my last respect to a dead man.

As I looked in the rear view mirror, I could see Angel lurking in the mist waiting for the hit to take place. I could see her making her way down the street with lights off. Then I pulled off, and made my way towards the game room. I was driving thinking to myself, if judging Dre was a good or bad idea. Then my phone rang! It was one of Dre's partners screaming in pain. He was shot several times in the chest. I acted like I was very emotional about the situation. I told him I had to pick up my family from the game room. Then I hung up! I hurried up and called Angel! She told me, I unloaded a chip of seventeen shots and hit him about six times in the chest. I told her that he was rushed to the hospital, but it looks bad for the home team. Then I would meet her at the game room, and we'll talk from there. I pulled up at the game room, and I could see my wife looking out the front door waiting on my arrival. She came to the car, and told me that she was very tired and needed some sleep. I asked if she was ready to go home and get some rest. Just stay in the car and I'll go get the kids. I started walking towards the game room, and I was greeted by Rodney. He stood there looking frustrated, because I was an hour behind schedule on his clock. I explained to him I was caught up in some amazing shit. So I'm sorry! Then walked on pass because I never had sorry in my blood, but he was doing me a favor. I could hear Ja'Cori and Trey laughing because of a video game they were playing. I called Trey! He turned around and looked at me, while blurting out daddy you going to make me lose. I stood there wondering how it felt to be free from all the destruction in the world. Then I thought about Randy in the car asleep. I told them to finish the game, and round up the wolf pack. I'll meet everyone at the car, because their mother was ready to lay down. I could see in both their faces a whole lot of pain, because they knew a good day had come to an end. Then I could hear someone calling my name. It was Angel! She came walking my way with a slight grin on her face. I knew what just happen was a piece of cake. She did a great favor for the streets! Angel explained as soon as I pulled up, I asked for Dre. By me being a female, he hurried up, and came towards the car. Out of excitement, he leans over and put his hands across the door ready to spit game. So I let him have it, with everything I had and more. All his so call friends just ran off, and left him for died like bitches. Then I smashed out to get far from the scene. I told her thank you, but it was time for me to get low. Plus, my wife is waiting in the car, and I need to take the kids home. After that I will go to the hospital to give my respects to Dre's family. Just the way Jam taught me on his table of life! I'll call you when I get things straight at home with my wife. But if not, I'll call you first thing in the morning. Therefore, we said our goodbye's! I turned and called for the kids! I stood there hoping everyone enjoyed their self today, but it was time to go home. I felt the love in the air, as they ran towards the vehicle. Randy was laying in the front seat fast asleep. So I asked Rodney to drive the other car to the house, because I didn't want to disturb my wife's nap. He stood there with a frown on his face for some reason. I asked him what was going on? He explained he needed someone to watch Rana in the morning. I told him that I would talk to him at the house, while all the boys loaded up in the car. Then after everyone got into the vehicles we drove off, and made our way towards the house. When we pulled up I felt safe without any worries in the world, because I was finally home. Then I leaned over and tapped my wife to let her know we were at home. I explained to her about Rodney's situation, and I said that we would watch Rana while he went to work. She smiled and I knew I had faith in my wife! I asked if he wanted to leave her, so he wouldn't have to rush in the morning for work. He looked at Rana while explaining what she needed to do tonight. She gave him a kiss then ran towards the house with Teedie and Toni. Rodney told us that he had a nice time, but he had to drive all the way across town. He knew it was a family thing, so we said our goodbyes and he went home. I looked at Randy in her hazel brown eyes, and told her that I had to run to the hospital. I need to check on Dre because he was shot tonight, and he's on life-support. I would be back in an hour or two, because I have to pay my respects to his family. I gave her a kiss, then made my way to the vehicle. I seen in my wife's eyes pain that was soon to explode, but I had to play the game raw. I could since that my wife was pissed off, but I had to stick to my plan. So I made my way towards the hospital, while Randy walked inside the house rubbing her eyes.

# CHAPTER 7

## Dealing With The Problem

As I made my way towards the hospital my phone rang. It was Angel! She explained that she was home alone until the morning, and if I wanted to stop by it would be ok. I told her that I would call her after I leave the hospital. I wanted to see if Dre was going to survive or die. When I walked into the hospital, I looked around for Dre's room. After I found it he was lying there with cords hanging from out his body. I felt sad, but he left me know choice. A doctor came to the waiting room and explained that his vital signs were set at 85 percent not to make it. He had a 15 percent chance to survive. It was up to God at this time! I walked out the room, and took a seat with his family. I sat there with a sad look on my face, and my head down to hide the pain. When I raise my head up there stood his mother! She stood there wondering why her only son was placed in this type of situation, while screaming in pain. I could feel all the pain, which dwelled throughout the hospital. I gave her a hug, while explaining that God will handle the rest upstairs. Minutes later, I could hear the sounds of the alarms going off, and I knew he was on his way to heaven or hell. I felt a cold breeze crawling in my skin, and I knew his days on earth was no more. Three doctors came from out his room with a disappointing look on their faces. Dr. Diaz approached his mother with a sad look on his face! He explained they did all they could do for her son. Dre's mother dropped to her knees with tears falling out her eyes crying why Lord why. I told his mother if she needed me I would be there in a flash. Here's my number, so call me if she needed anything. The number is 502-962-7118, and don't be afraid to call. Then I walked off with pain in my heart, because I just judged an old friend. I went a sat down in the car, because I had a bad vibe about what just happen. So I called Angel! I explained about Dre, and told her I was on my way to discuss the business. When I pulled up in front of her apartment. I seen Angel in the window, like a viper peeping my every move. As soon as I parked the vehicle, the apartment door swung open. I was greeted like a king! She explained that she was looking at the news, and the job was done professionally. There was not a trace of evidence left on the scene. As we walked into the house I took a seat on the couch. She asked me if I wanted something to drink? I relied with a beer if you have one please. She went into the kitchen to see what was to drink. I could hear her blurt out a Bud Ice fine with you Dee! Yes, that fine! I still was thinking of what just went down with Dre. I knew I couldn't turn back the hands of time, because everything happens for a reason. When she walked back into the room my head was hanging down. She knew it was because of me call a wild card call, and judged an old friend. I imaged if I was put in that situation how would everyone feel. I could hear her calling my name, trying to pull me out of the fucked up state of mind I was focus in. I felt her standing in front of me asking me why! I knew what happen, was now in the past. I felt what she was saying, but I was still confused. Then I could feel Satan working his way into my heart trying to wheel and deal. I explained to Angel how close me and Dre was before we became enemies. She started understanding the real truth, and why it had to be done. I told her about the police running in the spot. My friends were shot several times in the chest, because of Dre snitching. I couldn't let the weak link survive, because we weren't game like that. It hurt me to see our table fall apart, but shit happens for a reason. The strong will survive and the weak must die. Angel I open my heart to you, because I can see the real in you. Do u feel me Angel? Yeah I understand, but we have to take care of one another in this game. Yeah that's right! I need to run over Denise's house, so I can pick up at least a kilo of cocaine from out the trash. I better get there before someone finds it. Then I explained I would call in the morning to get the ball rolling. I turned and walked out the house to get in my vehicle. I sat in the car with my hands clutched on my forehead, because of the state of mind I was dwelling in. Then I was on my way to Denise's spot, where the 36 ounces lingered in the trash can in the backyard. I knew I had to be quick, fast, and alert to grab the product. Then bounce before being seen like a thief in the night. When I got to the area it felt strange and the lights were off on the whole streets. I started towards the back of the house, and I could see shells from a 9mm laying in the middle of the road. As I grew closer to the backyard, I began to think if everyone was still at the hospital with Dre's mother. I approached the backyard and there stood the trash can with the lid snuggled tight. I looked around to make sure I was not being peeped out. There laid two packages in the black bag. One kilo and 10 ounces of all pure cocaine! I quickly grabbed the shit and ran to the car to smash out like the wind. So I headed towards the house to hide the product. When I pulled in the front yard, I felt a loveable feeling lingering beyond the door. I walked inside the house, and I was greeted by Ja'Cori. He explained that he was waiting on me to return to tell me thank you for the special day. Standing there thinking a kid that has much respect, it hurt because everything could have gone down the other way. It could be me laying there instead of Dre. So I explained to him, it was my job son. I'll see you in the morning, because daddy needs some rest. He laughed while sipping on a cup of grape juice. Thomas and Trey back at it again on the video game in the bedroom. I just shut the bedroom door, and made my way towards my room. Randy laying there sound asleep at peace! I crawled into the bed slowly, so I wouldn't wake her from the relax dream she was having. I could feel my wife slowly making her way upon my chest. I explained I've been there! You looked very relax, so I let you sleep in peace. She gave me a kiss upon my neck, while explaining she love me with all her heart. So I return the favor and kissed her back. Then in other places, even between her light brown thighs and down below. As she went back to sleep, I laid there and began to dose off.

# CHAPTER 8

# *Calling in The Dogs*

I woke up at 7:15 am, from the sounds of my alarm clock to start a new day. I raised up looking around, because I was having a bad dream. I knew I couldn't let the guilt over power my way of thinking. The nightmares had to stop! The dark dreams felt so real! I crawled out the bed, and went into the bathroom to take a shower. I needed to wash off all the negative vibes, which dwelled over me. I stood in the shower, letting the hot water splash against my face to keep my body relax. When I started washing my face, I could hear Randy calling me to answer my cellular phone. I quickly dried off and made my way into my bedroom to get the phone. It was a missed call from Angel! So I called her to find out the business. She explained for me to meet her at the game room. I told her to meet me there in two hours, but please be on time while hanging up the phone. Randy standing there looking at the early news, and figuring out what really happen to Dre. It showed Dre had been shot, and how he got hit. She turned and looked at me, with a disappointed look on her face. She dropped to her knees crying in pain, because she knew it was me. I explained how I felt about my home-boys and Jam situation. This had to be done baby! If I let this situation pass I might be next on the menu. Then I walked pass my wife with hell racing from my veins, because of her feeling sorry for an expired enemy. I walked back into the bathroom, and I could see Randy in the mirror with her hands on her face crying. I slowly entered the room, and explained to my wife I was sorry for snapping at her. I said everything in the wrong way baby, but Dre got Turtle and De' Shot killed. It could be me laying there instead of them, because he was seeking power. I could see the pain all over her face, because she felt like friends wouldn't kill each other over money. Money, cocaine, nor power, is not the situation between us baby. Plus, a snitch must die! I wish I lived another lifestyle, but I'm in to deep. I can't fall weak sweetie in this dirty game. Do you understand, how I have to live in these fucked up streets? I wish I could turn the other way in life, but it's too late for me. She dropped her head and started crying again, because the things I was talking about were real feelings. She got up and walked pass me without saying a word. Then went and laid on the bed with a painful look on her face. She asked if I like living as a drug dealer? I didn't want to answer the question! I just looked up wondering what if I was living a regular lifestyle. So I bent down and put my arms around my wife's neck, while giving her a kiss upon the lips. I started telling her about the life I use to live before I became a hustler. I was a square jo that lived by my mother's rules. She pulled me close, while telling me she loved me with all her heart. Then my cellular rang again, and it was Angel. She asked if Diamond could join the click? I explained that it was up to her, but I hope she has heart. Because the weak must die on this table we revolve around. Then Angel explained if her sister fell weak, she would be the one to clean up the mess in blood. Then we both hung up the phone, so we could get ready! I felt my power in the streets was growing like a disease. If I kept to the plan, people would start to fear us as drug dealers. I sat there looking at my wife, but I had to think fast. I explained I need her to deposit some money into the bank. She just laughed! I asked her what was so funny? She explained for me to look out the window, because Woo and Muff were stuck and needed to be pulled apart. I smiled and went to take care of the job. A bucket of very hot water would do the job and break them apart. I could see the frustration flowing from both dogs. So I walked in between both their ass, and let the hot water do the trick. They spite apart and ran like, I was trying to hurt them both. I could hear my wife laughing from the house loud, because how the dogs departed from one another. I could hear someone calling me from the house. It was Capri! She asked where was Randy? I explained she was in the bedroom, and do you have something good for today? She just smiled, while blurting out you know it man. She showed me some white rhino, and gave me a blunt that was already rolled. I could tell that the weed was the killer. I sat there thinking if I should fire it up before I went to meet the twins. So I fired it up anyway! I felt the smoke hover through my flesh. My eyes felt like weights, but very hard to keep open. I knew I was high, but still I had to continue as plan. I was so high I felt like going back to bed to let it wear off, but I still had to stay focus on my agenda. However, plotting on my next move in life as a sinner. Then I called two of my friends that lived in the country. Rabbit and Nut Bush! I felt if I called them it would be a problem in the streets. Nut answered the phone and immediately asked what was the problem. I explained it has been along crazy week for me. He knew I was talking in code words, because I didn't like talking over the phone about business. I heard Rabbit in the background asking if I was ok? I told Nut I needed them to come see me. They explain it was a done deal, and everything was being set as a dark arrival. Then we both hung up the phone! I knew in my heart I could depend on these two, because we were like family. Then I explain to Randy I had to take care of some business. I gave her a kiss then turned around to make my way towards the door. I got into the vehicle and went to the game room. When I pulled up I was greeted by the twins. Angel standing in front of Diamond waiting on my arrival. I asked if they were hungry or wanted something to drink? Angel respond with no thanks, while Diamond stood there smiling. I knew these two females were dangerous together. I could tell they would get the job done, without a doubt. Diamond explained we could set up shop over her house. I sat there wondering to myself, because Diamond was a new fish on the table. I knew everything would fall together as planned. I explained to both of them, let's get rich or die trying. It's time to take over the streets with a devilish look on my face. Angel could feel the fire which lingered throughout my negative soul. I knew that all the fun days were over, and now it was time to set pain into the streets. So we made our way towards the vehicles, so we could meet over Diamonds house. We loaded up in both cars, and went towards Diamonds spot to take care of business. When we pulled up it was a nice place to set up shop. I knew everything was set to go down as planned. They walked towards the house, while I trailed behind watching our every move. In my heart I was placed in front of two females who would be in my corner until the bitter end. Everything started to fall in play! So I went into the kitchen and started getting my things out to work with. I weighted ounce by ounce, while distributing 5 ounces to them both. I told them 3,600 was to be brought back to me. We all agreed! Then my phone rang, and it was Randy! She wanted to know if I was going to be all night? She wanted to go over to her mother's house with the kids. I let her know I would be home soon, and to be ready waiting on my arrival. I hung up the phone, and got back to business. Angel and Diamond knew that I loved my wife, and I would do anything for the family. I could sense the both of them had been dealt a bad hand in life. Things were going to get better for the both of them once this matter was over and done with. After the business deal was done, I knew I had to meet my family. So I let them both know to call me, and stay in touch. Then

I made my way the vehicle, so I could go home. This was to cheer up my wife, and give a little support to the family life. When I got home, I could feel peace in the air. As I entered the house I could hear Randy soft voice calling out my name. I ask her was she ready to go and get everything started? As we made our way to the car, I knew she had something to say. On the way to her mother's house, she wanted to know about Dre's family situation. I told her that I really couldn't explain anything right now. It was a lot going on at the moment, and I didn't want to keep involving people especially my wife. I let her know that once things were cleared I'd sit down and explain everything to her. She nodded with her head, while leaning back in the seat and close her eyes. She kept her eyes close until we arrived at her mother's house. I could tell she was bothered, because I didn't explain anything about the Dre situation. Once we arrived at her mothers, I knew she would get her mind off things. So I kissed her on the lips letting her know she had nothing to worry about. As we made our way inside her mother's house, Mrs. Skinner was sitting in the rocking-chair reading the Bible. She was happy to see that we had made it on time for the family get together. I asked if she was doing ok? She just smiled and continued to rock in the chair, while reading the Bible. Randy gave her a hug, then walked in the kitchen to see what was cooking. The kids went straight out the back door to play, and see their grandfather. So I sat down on the couch asking Randy to get me something to drink. Her mother started to talk to me about the Lord. The things she spoke came straight out the Bible. When my wife returned with the drink, I was almost in tears. Her conversation was so deep; I couldn't hardly drink anything! My mouth was bone dry, But Randy knew she had my undivided attention. She was glad I was listening to something other than the street life stuff. I was so thirsty, dehydration kept running through my mind. I finally drank my drink! Randy laughing her ass off, because she knew how thirsty I was in the beginning but I didn't want to be rude. After our spiritual talk, she asked if we were hungry? She went into the kitchen telling Randy to get the kids ready, so they could eat, Seconds later, I heard the back door open, and in came the kids with Randy's father. Everyone went into the bathroom to wash their hands, and came back to sit at the table for their grandmother's meal. As we were saying our grace, the aroma from the food was making me hungry as hell. Then everyone began to pig-out! After the long meal, I knew it was getting late and the kids had school in the morning. Randy explained, she had a nice time, but it was time to put the kids to bed. So we said our goodbyes, while walking towards the family vehicle. On our way home I could feel my wife was in a great mood, but it was soon to change. When we made it home, I was happy as hell. I just wanted to lay in the bed to get some sleep, because I was full like a stuff turkey. When I made it to my bedroom, Randy was coming from the bathroom with a grin on her face. So I laid back with my hands across my chest thinking freaky thoughts. She crawled into the bed, and laid next to me talking about the family situation. She asked if I had something to wear? I respond with no in a slick way then laughed. My wife knew I was lying! I had something to wear for every occasion. Then I heard a loud noise! It was Rika, which was a live caddy piece that was very sweet. She came in with the jokes! She explained she needed someone to follow her to drop off the car over her brother's house. Randy got fully dressed and explained for me to be ready when she got back. I stood there nodding my head side to side, because I was pissed off. Rika blurted out things get better in due time Dee, while making her way toward the car. I felt like she knew about the Dre situation. So I went into the bathroom, and stood in front of the mirror to think to myself. I knew a lot of negative energy was running through the room that made me nervous. I could see another side of myself in a dark way. A person who had feelings for the world, but lived in a dark world of pain and destruction. I turned on the shower and got in to take a hot bath, so I could wash off the sinful feels that stood in my way. After taking the shower I got dressed! Then I sat on the edge of the bed, with my head hanging down. Thomas came in the bedroom and ask me if I was ok? I explained I was fine and needed some time to myself to focus on a situation. He seen that I was fine, so he walked out! The love for me was there, and he didn't want nothing less from his father. After I finished getting dressed my phone rang. It was Angel! She explained a friend needed four and a half ounces of all raw powder. He had 3,200 to spend! I told her to keep him around, and I'll meet them at the game room in a half hour. Then we both hung up the phone! I weighted the 126 gram of cocaine, so I could have it ready for the buyer. Minutes later I could hear Randy walking through the door discussing parts about the stories of All My Children. I told her I had to make a drop, and her smile went to a frown. She knew I had to make the drug transaction, but she didn't care because it was family time. I said I would be back in a flash. Rika explained to Randy that we have plenty time, so let him handle his business and be safe. I could feel that the words were strong enough to make my wife understand. So I went to take care of my business with Angel.

# CHAPTER 9

# Taking Care of Business

I called the twins to explain to them that I was short on time. Plus, I needed everything to go down as planned. So meet me at the game room as soon as possible. When I pulled up at the game room, I seen Angel standing in front of her vehicle, and Diamond coming from out the game room peeping whatever moved. I knew everything was clear when I arrived. Angel gave me the 3,200, while I laid the drugs on the front seat of the car. She stood there looking into her eyes like something was wrong. I told them to be safe, and I'd get with them a little later. I had to get home to my wife and kids. As I turned and walked to my vehicle. I thought about some crazy shit on my way home. I knew if a male or a female tried to get in my way, they'd be left frozen in their own blood. I called my wife to let her know I'd be home in 5 to 10 minutes' tops. As I pulled up into the driveway, I could see my wife kneeling down planting flowers. I asked her how long have she been on her knee's, giving life to these flowers. She said with a loud remark, a flower is one of the most precious things in life. They grow to be beautiful and has its own distinctive smell. After having the flower discussing, I went into the house to see Alicia and Ashley. Making their way towards me, I could hear them saying they were invited to a swimming party with a friend. Can we go daddy? The party is tonight over a friend's house. I told them to ask their mother, but it was ok with me. This would give me and my wife some quality time together. I made my way into the kitchen to get me a cold beer. Rika walked pass me blurting out, you and Randy need to get yawl shit together. I stood there laughing, because I didn't know where this conversation was leading too. Nor did I know where it was going, so I sipped on my Bud Ice, rubbing my head thinking what was going on. Rika never said anything else, just looking at the both of us. I had an idea, but I didn't want to get into it. I already had a lot on my mind, and that would be something else to think about. I told Randy our family cook out was getting ready to start in 45 minutes, and for her to get ready. She told me that the girls were riding with her and the boys with me. I stood there amazed because I was thinking we were going to ride together as a family. So I called the boys! I told them to meet me at the car, because I didn't want to be late. I could hear the arguing of the front seat at the car. So I made my way to the vehicle to see what was all the commotion about. I made them all get in the back seat to stop all the shit. I told Trey and Thomas that they were brothers. It wasn't supposed to be fighting with each other because they were family. The silence in the car on the way to the family get together was special, but they'll be alright. I let them know they were all loved the same, but Ja'Cori and Brandon should've knew better because they were older. When we arrived we all were greeted by Rabbit and Nut Bush! I asked them when did they get in town? Rabbit said we been here since this morning. The look in their eyes was hell on wheels. I could tell they were up to know good. I tried to tell them why I ask them to come to the Ville. It has been one cat giving me problems in the street. This is some spooky shit! I know that I have business to handle, and I need these chills to go away. So I need Taz touched! The deal was set and I needed to find Randy. So I followed behind Rabbit, and we ran into Capri. Her eyes were blood shot red, and I knew she was on something good. So I asked what she was smoking? She pulled out a bag of purple haze! After she rolled the blunt and fired it up, I knew it was time to zone out. Still she acts like it was her last one to smoke, because she had a problem with passing the weed. When she passed it to me, I could see Randy, Rika, and Alicia walking my way with a sad look on their faces. I didn't know what to say, so I waited on the question that was getting ready to be asked. Randy explained she forgot to stop and pick up the drinks. So I told her I would go to the liquor store, and purchase some Crown to get the night started. I was high as hell trying to focus on my wife, and what she wanted to drink. Alicia just laughed because she knew I was high and off balance. Then I made my way towards the vehicle, so I could go get the drinks. I got into the car and made my way towards the liquor store. When I got there it was a lot of movement in the area, and didn't feel safe. After getting the Crown and Don P, I made my way back to the vehicle. Outside I knew life was getting out of control! There stood Taz and a couple of his friends, who lived in a world of sin. These cats were no joke, and didn't take shit! So I kept walking towards the car, but I had a bad feeling that I was being peeped out. Walking pass Taz, I heard him call out my name! So I stop and turn back around! He explained that he was sorry about the situation with Dre. I knew that I was next on someone's menu, so I had to think fast. I told him thank you for the support, and I quickly got into my vehicle to leave the negative area. However, I had to keep my eyes on the rearview mirror, to making sure I wasn't being trailed. Then I got back to the family gathering, and I could see my wife walking from out the mist towards me. She could see that something was on my mind, but right now wasn't the time nor place. I was there to have fun with the family! I asked Randy were was Capri? I was getting ready to go get her, but she was making her way towards me. I asked her what was shacking? Then she responded with are yawl ready. Then take this blunt and fire it up Dee! I took the blunt and lit it, and I could feel the rich weed smoke rolling through my lungs. What I was mad about was blowing away in smoke in seconds. As I passed the blunt to my wife, I could feel my spirits lifting up. Then she leaned over and gave me a kiss on my forehead, while thanking me for the drinks. After getting high, I turned and walked away looking for Nut and Rabbit. They both were standing by the grill getting a bite to eat. So I walked over and explained the shit that just went down at the store. Rabbit blurted out, why didn't you have someone to ride with you to the store. Right now you're a sitting duck without security! One slip and you will be laying there next to your home-boy's. Then Nut explained they had to get Taz sooner than expected. I could feel painful thoughts running through Nut eyes, and I knew that the street life was about to pick up. Then I turned around and went to look for my wife. When I saw her she was sitting on the porch with Capri and Rika feeding her face. I told her I had to make a stopover Angel's house before I went home. I could see the expression on my wife's face, like stopping over her house wasn't a good idea. My business was involve, so I had no choice at all. I asked her if she wanted to ride with me! She gave me a fucked up look, like don't play with me right now. So I took that as a yes! So go asked Rika, if she could take the kids home, because it will be too late to run back and forward. As she stood there with a grin on her face, I wondering how life would really be if I was to give this lifestyle up for good. All the family members were still having the time of their life. I asked Capri to bring me a Bud Ice! She went to get the drink, but she knew I was going through something besides the family get together. My cellular began to ring! It was Diamond! Our job is done! Speaking loudly into my ear, I just stood there with a grin on my face. Happy as hell the transaction was safe, without any blood being shed. Two females running through 280 grams of cocaine in a flash.

My timing was off because I was still having fun with our family. Before ending my call with the two of them, I asked were they ok? Yes, but tired and ready to go home. I told them to meet me at the spot and we both hung up. I was seeing things were beginning to come alive. At the same time my life was headed somewhere I didn't want it to be. Being hungry was starting to distract me from life itself, and I felt Satan moving in. that was the part I didn't want to involve my wife in. Selling drugs was going to bring on extra problems, and I had a lot on the line. It was time to get away for a while so, I asked Randy did she want to take a vacation? She stood there with a surprise look on her face. Where are we going she asked? I was like how about Florida! Yes, she responded, and when are we leaving. I told her as soon as possible! I made my way to meet the twins at the spot, and Rika will drive the kids home as planned. When I got to the spot I explained to them both about my plans of the vacation with my wife. They thought that it would be a great idea for me to get away on a trip. I would be gone a week, so I was hoping things would stand still until I returned. Knowing my two sidekicks would be holding it down without a doubt. So I continued to discuss the business with them both, so I could get home to my kids. After taking care of the deal me and Randy headed home. She wanted to know exactly when she could make reservations to Florida. I let her know it would be in a couple days. She was already thanking me in her soft sexy voice. I nodded my head thinking this trip is really what we both needed at the time. When we arrived at home, I had Rabbit and Nut to come over. Rabbit was trying to holler at my girl Rika, but nothing was happening. She was like I don't need a dealer in my life. We just started laughing because they weren't dealers they were killers. Nut was like what's going on? We'll I been hearing some very disturbing news on the streets, and it involves Taz. He needs to be knocked ASAP! The news isn't good I explained! Rabbit asked where does he stay and what side of town? Out South in the projects I explained. Look this has to be a clean job. I can't afford any slips! You know Ayanna is his gal, and she be having his back at a hundred percent. I got his ass Nut nodded! I felt he had something crazy running through his mind, because he kept rubbing his chin. He explained Ayanna was a female he messed with before moving to the country. I knew the Taz situation was going to be an easy hit, because he would persuade her into setting him up. Everything was going to be handled in the right manner, a person could never imagine. Rabbit just smiled and I could feel Taz was getting ready to get it. Nut blurted out I got you Dee! We'll call you when the job is done. I just nodded my head and grin. After everything was set I went into the house to get some dream action in the bed, while they got down to business.

# CHAPTER 10

# *Getting Down to Business*

The next morning, I wanted to spend some time with the Family. I asked Randy if her and the kids would like to go to the movies? Yes, she replied! She called to see when the movie was playing, while I got dressed for the occasion. When she came into the bedroom, she told me what time the movie started. Today seem like a good day to spend quality time with the family. The movie started at 12:45pm sharp, so we were rushed for time. I asked if the kids were ready, and meet me at the car? As I walked to the vehicle, I wondered if Nut and rabbit plan was going to work. Minutes later, I seen the kids making their way towards the family vehicle with my wife. Once everyone was inside the van, I made my way toward the movie theater. When we arrived I had 15 minutes to purchase the tickets, and get the kids their snacks. After getting the popcorn and candy we went to take our seats. However, waiting on the movie to start, I thought about the Taz situation. As the movie began, I could feel my kids were enjoying it, while my wife sat there thinking about something. I didn't want to ask her what was on her mind, so I continued watching the movie. After the movie was over, I asked if everyone had a good time? Yes, they all replied! On our way home, I could hear the kid's discussion the scenes from the movie. They were happy we had family day together, but still my mind was focused on the Taz situation. I could feel that my wife had a lot on her mind, but I didn't want our kids hearing any of our debates. I was trying very hard to picture what was really on her mind at this time, but I couldn't imagine. As I pulled up into the driveway, I noticed our gate was opened wide. I went to the back hatch to pull out my 9mm just to be safe. While walking towards the backyard, I could tell that someone had been trying to break in the back door, but didn't succeed. Both dogs had been barking crazy, but calmed down once they seen their master. I unchained the both of them, so that they could run around, and sniff things out before my family went into the house. I went inside the house with my mind made up to kill or be killed. This matter was involving my family. A little too close for comfort, if you ask me! After storming through the house, I made sure it was safe for my family to come in. I called for Randy! When she came in the house, I already knew things were going to be heated between the both of us because of my lifestyle. She knew I was the reason why someone tried to break in the house. She walked around yelling, like it was my fault this shit a cared. While she stormed through the house with an attitude, I explained to her what happen was a part of life. Plus, life isn't no cookies and cream! Then I went into the bedroom, and sat on the edge of the bed thinking about this problem. I knew things like this came with the game, which I revolved around as a drug dealer. Randy tried to explain, she was sorry for jumping the gun, because things could happen like this anywhere. I knew this was going to be some tough shit to swallow, but I still was confused about what just went down at my house. So I got up and went into the bathroom to take a piss! I heard her called my name, but I had a lot of shit on my mind. So I didn't respond! When I came from out the bathroom, I went to check on the stash spot, which my wife knew nothing about. There laid one kilo of cocaine tied tight in the black bag, sitting on the top shelf. Once Randy seen me standing there with the product, she blurted out is that what they were out to get. Then she walked off with an angry look on her face, because she felt I was putting everyone in harm's way. So I quickly grabbed my phone and called Angel! As I explained what just happen, she told me to get the drugs to the safe house. Then she said my flight for Florida was set for 7:45pm tomorrow night. I told her to grab the loose ends, and meet me at Denny's. I would be inside getting me a bite to eat, so call me when yawl arrive. I'll bring the drugs to the car, so we can make the exchange like a hit and run. Then we both hung up the phone, so I could tell my wife what I needed to do. I explained, I had to go make a big drop off, and it contained some big money. She just blurted out fine, while walking away with hell racing through her body. I stood there puzzled, because of the negative comment from my wife. So I just grabbed the product from the closet, and headed to my vehicle to get the job done. As I started the car, I felt a lot of pain, which was cluttering my heart. Because my wife was on another page! On my way towards Denny's I felt shit was coming to a head, and things was soon to hit the fan. As I pulled up at Denny's it seems to be a quiet place to meet, because I didn't feel that negative vibe. I still took my safety off the 9mm, while I made my way into the restaurant too get a bite to eat. As I took my seat, a nice sweetie female with the eyes of a Goddess took my order. After placing my order, I felt the twins were growing near, so the deal could take place. Then my phone began to ring, and it was Angel! She said they were pulling up into the Denny's parking lot. So I got up and went to greet the two female vipers, with the package. Angel responded with, thank you Dee for a chance to prove our self to this table of life. Then gave me a hug, while pausing like she wanted to give me a kiss. I could since what was in my presents, was a female who was slowly falling in love with a drug dealer. After the deal was made I explained, I would need a ride to the airport an hour early to be safe. Angel knew of the situation, while her sister standing there with a surprise face. So I went ahead and give her the rundown of what was going on in the streets. I knew the product was being placed in the right hands, but it was time for me to take a break away from the streets for a few days. After the product was careful secured inside the vehicle, we made our way into Denny's to grab a bite to eat. I sat at the table in a deep thought thinking about the problem, that just went down at home between me and my wife. I wondered why someone tried to break into our residence, and violated my family privacy. I had a great suspense, that Taz knew something about the violation of my home. As the waiter brought us our food. Angel asked if I needed anything else done in the streets before I board the plane to Florida. I knew what was written on her face signaled pain, but was willing to get the job done immediately. I wanted to call the wild card shot, but Nut and Rabbit were already set on that mission. So I explained to the twins that their plate was full, because these two ladies had plenty of product to get off. Then I sparked a conversation about Angel's new friend Jay. She said he lived downtown, but he would love to get on the money train. So why did you ask me about him she replied? I need him to drive around the city serving my customers so everyone would think I'm still in town. Do you all understand what I'm trying to say ladies? Both of them responded yes, with a surprise look on their faces. This is why I need everything to go down as I planned. Diamond blurted out, do you feel someone else is trying to war against our table of life. I don't know sweetie, but it's some strange shit going down. I have a gut feeling that I'm right. Therefore, I need this table to be ready, if some dumb shit does pop off. So this is the deal! I don't even want my wife to know about this disappearing act, which is going to take place. What they responded! I told them both to calm down, and don't take this in the wrong way. I feel there is someone slick in the game, and I'm trying my best to stay ahead. So I need you to get in touch with Jay, so we can get the ball rolling. This will give us some time to find out all the loose links, and what was really going down in the streets. I have had a bad feeling that someone has signed on the dotted line with Satan himself. So right now, I have to take light steps! I need yall to listen this time without any questions. I can still keep the narcotics on the streets, but everyone needs to be on the same page. So it's best for Jay to run around for me, and let him catch the hell from the streets. I want to see the enemy from a distance, and bring out the mystery motherfucker that wants me dead. I know it's something fishy in the water, and we all need to be ready with our guards up. So Angel get in touch with Jay, and get him ready for his starring position. The twins just stood there laughing! Angel I'm leaving you in charge of the whole operation. Yes, she explained! I've called an old friend who lives in Miami by the name of Telvin. He's from Memphis on the north side of town, but now in Florida doing his pimping thing. I let him know, I needed to come down there for a while until things blow over. He was upset, because we go back a long way in life. From hoe's calling him pimp and me player. Angel knew this would be a hard task, but she was skilled by the best. I felt she fit the position which needed to be played, and the ball was in her court. I wanted everyone to think I was still ding my thing, but out of sight out of mind. I needed this shit nipped in the bud as soon as possible. After the conversation about Jay, I explained that Telvin would be at the airport waiting on my arrival. Then my phone began to ring, and it was my wife! She asked if I was alright? Yes, I replied. I told her I would be home in a hour or two. Hear in my wife's voice a lot of pain, because she wanted to know my location. I had a strange feeling, so I lied about my true location. Then I blurted out, I love you sweetie while hanging up the phone. The twins stood there looking at me with a surprise look on their faces. I could feel that the females could see the state of mind, which I was being placed in without a doubt. I told Angel that she needed to get Jay to play smart ball in the streets, and keep his mouth closed at all times. She responded, and if it isn't closed I will close it myself, with a slight frown on her face. I told them after I eat this meal, I need to make my way home to the family. So everything looks good in my favor! Therefore, after the nice meal, I got up and paid for my service. Then gave the waitress a tip that really caught her eye. as we made way to the vehicles, I began to think about what was next on the agenda. I knew everything was set up, and it was time to play a game of cat and mouse. I told everyone bye and pulled off into the mist to make my way home. When I arrived at the house, I was greeted at the door by my wife. She explained, the family get together was tomorrow night. I told her that I would have everything ready for the gathering, but I had some big things going down. I had to pick up a quantity of drugs for my table of life. I might have to sit and wait on their arrival. So it might take a day or two before I return. I could feel a lot of anger coming from off my wife's chest., but this had to be done. Therefore, I made my way into the bedroom, and laid across the bed with my hands behind my head thinking about the twins situation. I knew Angel had her hands full, but Jay's situation was small to a giant. She had the eyes, which could hypnotize a person on site like a king cobra. Then I could hear Randy making her way towards the back room. When she crawled into bed, I could see that she had been crying about our family situation. She started talking about our ongoing relationship as husband and wife. She said, it was hard raising the kids on her own, while their father ran the streets selling drugs. I stopped her in her tracks, baby you have to accept the good and the bad. I know you like to spend money. Therefore, I have to re-up and build up what was lost. Then I rolled over and gave her a kiss on her sexy fine lips. As she expressed to me that she understood, I slowly undressed her until she laid there naked. I slid between her legs, and began to lightly lick around the belly button, while making my way towards them cupcakes. Then I began to suck on her breast as if I was eating icing off a cake. She started to rub her fingers though my braids, while moaning and groaning out of ecstasy calling out my name. I was thrusting myself between her legs as I swung my champ like never before. I knew I was giving her body what it needed to relax, because the nails dug deeper into my sweaty back like she was a tiger. As the sweat trickled down my face, like I was in a rain storm the more I swung the champ. She proceeded to lick the sweat off my neck and shoulder because she was loving the feeling of the hot sex. I could see the pain and pleasure lingering in and out her face, because of the foreplay. As she whispered sensual words in my ear, while telling me she didn't want me to live. This through off my whole rhythm, so I stopped having sex and rolled over with hands behind my head. She laid there pissed off, because the love making had come to an end. I began concentrating on something else. I began explaining, about the situation of the street life. As I tried to confide in her, I knew everything I said was going into one ear and out the other. So I got up and went into the bathroom and stood in front of the mirror contemplating about the twins and minutes later, I turned around then walked into my bedroom, while sitting on the edge of the bed starring at Randy for a moment, I could see her laying there with hell racing from her body. I was a side of my wife, that I've never seen before during our whole relationship. I just laid back down, but I felt a bad vibe while lying down beside her. I grabbed my wife and pulled her close to me, while gazing into her dark brown eyes asking what was wrong? At the same time, I was trying to cheer her up, and put a smile on her face. She explained, how everything should be n as a family. I knew telling her about going out of town was a bad idea. I had to think fast, and plan another escape. So I could catch the booked flight on time without a doubt. I quickly asked her if she wanted to go to the movies again, so she could clear her mind? She sat up on the bed and asked when! Tomorrow about three pm, is that cool? She said okay! I told her I hope we can get over all the negative shit that is currently destroying our marriage, because I love to see you happy. You are my wife, but still I live in a dark world of selling drugs. I knew everything I planned had to go down without my wife knowing the business. Then I reached for my phone, while walking outside to call Angel. I told her about my flight to Florida, and I needed her to have Jay on the up and up. Because my wife was on my ass. She doesn't need to know anything about this plan. I need her to think I'm running around taking care of my business elsewhere Angel. She replied, I feel you Dee, but still I don't know why. I need you to focus only on Jay, so every move is precise. I know this will be a hard task, but I need this to go down in the best way. This will make everyone in the city think Jay is me. I have already called Telvin, and he'll be waiting on my arrival. Just call me in the morning when you pick up Jay. I'll meet you at the game room, and we'll get the ball rolling from there. After talking to Angel I walked into the house, and crawled back in the bed with my wife. She was lying there wondering what was going on. I gave her a kiss then turned over to go to sleep, so I could prepare for tomorrow grand adventure. This was a master plan, so I laid there with my eyes closed trying to fake sleep. I could feel my wife's hand making its way across the middle of my chest. The soft voice of my wife, asking if I was still awake. As if she was still horny from the earlier episode. Therefore, I never said a word, because I wanted this day to end. An hour of lying down I still, could feel myself drifting into a deep sleep.

# CHAPTER 11

## *Love in the Air*

The next morning, I wake up hearing my boy's voice arguing about a damn video game. So I made my way into their bedroom. Low and behold, it was Thomas and Brandon fighting like dogs tangled up at war with one another. I busted into the room and stopped them from fighting. I loudly explained, brother don't fight they are supposed to guard each other with their life. I could see that Satan had been rebuked from the room as they both smiled. As I walked back into my bedroom, she was getting ready for her set plans of the day. I asked if she was going to the bank to withdraw some money, so we could prepare for our journey. I knew deep in my heart that my timing was everything, because I had a flight to catch. I grabbed my cellular phone off the dresser and made my way to the front door of the house. I called Angel and I could hear a male's voice. It was jay! I knew the twins were already on the move, and shit was being conducted at its best in life. I asked Angel to rebook my flight for later, and to call me after it was done. I informed her that I had made plans with my family, and I had to erase my every step to get free. I had only one shot to vanish from my wife, so I can find out who really wants me dead. Then I hung up the phone, and went back inside the house. Randy was sitting at the table sipping on some coffee. I could tell that something was on her mind, but she kept it to herself. I asked her if she would go to the bank to get some cash, so we could get our day started right away. Then I proceeded to go into the bedroom to change clothes, so we could get right down to business as a family. As I was getting dressed I could hear her walking out the front door and starting the car. After getting dressed I wondered to myself if I needed to pack my 9mm, because I could feel a negative vibe throughout the house. So I grabbed my firearm and stuck it in the back of my pants to be safe. Twenty minutes had passed, then I heard my wife pulling up in the driveway. I had everything ready so we could get the special day rolling as a family adventure. I met her at the door, but she had this painful look on her face. I just acted as if I didn't peep the frown, because I already had a lot set on my plate at this time. As we went to the vehicle, I pulled the gun out and placed it under the seat. I looked up and I saw my wife and kids making their way towards the car. I asked her if she was ok? She said yeah! I could still tell that something was bothering her, so I just leaned back in the seat to get comfortable and prepared for the ride. My phone began to ring and it was Angel! She explained, everything was ready to go down at a hundred percent. Jay is willing to start his starring position! So I explained, this was not the right time for us to discuss any business, because my family was in the car. Angel could tell that my wife was in my presence, and I couldn't respond to the questions she was asking me. I told her I would call soon as we got to our destination, and then I hung up the phone. I could see in Randy's eyes, that she was wondering what my business call was all about. When we arrived at our destination, I got out of the vehicle and stood by it. I could feel a real strange vibe that gave me the chills, because it felt like someone was getting ready to take me out. I looked around wondering why I was afraid, while my family walked into the entrance of the movie theater. I stood there thinking to myself, if my day to be judged was growing near. So I grabbed my cellular phone off the seat and called Angel. I explained, I need her and Jay to meet me at the game room in one hour. I hung the phone up and made my way into the theater. When I spotted my family, I asked Randy if she had paid for the tickets? She just looked at me with an evil look from hell like I did something wrong. Right then I knew something strange was in the air. She then handed me a ticket, and walked away towards the show. I followed behind just thinking to myself, why she didn't give me a kiss, hug, nor any kind of love affection. I felt as if life was at a standstill, but I knew I had to meet Angel in exactly one hour. I sat down to watch the movie, and it started off with a love scene. I started thinking to myself, that this movie reminded me of our relationship. Then my phone began to vibrate and it was Angel! She informed me that they would be at the game room in ten minutes. I whispered ok, and that I would be there as soon as I could. As I hung up the phone, I sat there beside my wife in deep thought contemplating how I was going to play this off. Then a brilliant idea popped in my head, so I called Rodney! He was daze because he knew something was up, but there was money involved. I explained, I needed a ride and to where! He was on his way like a flash of light! Fifteen minutes later I could see him looking around for me. As I walked over to greet him, I told him to tell Randy you need help on the project. He told the lie well and nodded ok, while we made our way toward his vehicle. I explained, we need to meet Angel at the game room ASAP. We were on our way to meet a friend at the game room. When we arrived, I could see Angel blending in with the cars like a chameleon in its own surroundings. When I greeted her, she began to discuss the likes and dislikes about the Jay situation. She said that Jay was cool, but he thought he was the shit. I told her that he is the shit! Plus, I needed him for that same reason, and I know that the shit is going to hit the fan soon. I just wanted him to play his cards right to draw in the shooter. Now let's go meet Jay! I could feel the fear which dwelled within the car because I had his attention. As I opened the door and climbed in to introduced myself to Jay. I explained, how everything needed to take place while I was out of town. I let him know it's a lot of money involved. I could see in his eyes that I had a new friend who wanted to join the team, be his job was temporary. After the short conversation of his job instructions, I exited the vehicle. Angel sat there with a frown on her face, because my next move was to catch my flight to Florida. I told her I would call them as soon as my plane landed in Miami. Then I explained for them to be safe, and let Jay for fill his position on the team. As I made my way towards Rodney's car, I asked him to take me to the airport and I'll give him two hundred for his time. I made it very clear to him, that I didn't want anyone to know nothing. Not even my wife! He understood the words that was coming from out my mouth. Then I got out the car, and went to board the plane. I walked up to the clerk and asked when does the Miami plane depart from the Ville. She explained, it would be boarding in thirty minutes and in the air in forty. It would be a two-hour flight, then I got my reserved ticket and took a seat. Twenty minutes came to pass and I heard the alarm to board the plane. I felt frighten feelings flowing through my body, because I was scared of heights. So I found my numbered seat which was on the ticket, and put my seatbelt on tight. As the plane took flight I could feel the tribulation of the plane in the clouds that scared me shitless. Still the fight was a peace of mind, which I really needed at that this time. Hours later, the plane was on its way to Florida, so I could kick it with an old friend. As the plane began to land after a long trip in the air, we made it safe to Miami. A place where I was labeled a nobody, plus I didn't have any enemies in this state. So I made my way to the phone booth, so I could give Telvin a call. Then I could hear someone calling my name out loud. It was Telvin! He was standing with his hands crossed, and four hoes from different nature by his side. I was greeted with it is P! That's short for player! Say man, what been going on in the Ville? Nothing but the same shit, and I see your lifestyle been good. I see you put on some weight, and some new horses in the stable. Yeah man! When I was in the Ville, I said I didn't want nothing black but a Cadillac. However, a snow bunny was my for show money that will walk me through this storm. Since I been in Florida, I've been impressed by the black cat. This was short for black hoes! O by the way! I said I was going to purchase me a European hoe, and I did player. You will see when we get to the pimp palace, because I got all kinds of flavored ice-cream at home. I had to get away to find out the bad vibe that was on my chest. Then we started making our way to his vehicle. He was driving a H-2 Hummer! He explained, pimps ride in the front, and the hoes ride close by the trunk. Then smiled while getting in the truck. He started the vehicle, while telling the hoes who I was. The hoes were excited to see another male figure, who contain the same game but a different lifestyle. I knew that everything that I was about to get into was going to be fun. When we arrived at the pimp palace it felt like a whole new world. It was hoes everywhere walking around naked taking care of business, trying to make sure he was happy. I was in heaven! Females greeting me with great wellness, but Sunshine was a game Pitt. She stood 6 feet 2 inches with green emerald eyes, long blond hair, and thick as gumbo. I felt like it was sex ready to get fucked by a Louisville player. I explained to Telvin that his house was nice, and the hoes made it even better. He just grinned while walking into the house giggling! He had some shit planned for us to get into tonight, but I was still focused on my home town situation. Then I explained, about the shit that was going down in the Ville. Taz was from New York, and he was causing me a problem in the streets. Don't worry because he's headed to the meat wagon in due time. I was worried about some more shit, that was making me have these deep thoughts. I feel someone close to me is trying to track me down, and I don't know why. This is why I'm down here, and I got a chance to find out who really wants me dead. So when I find out! I want revenge and someone else is going to die. Then he gave me a tour around the pimp palace. I felt I was in a safe area, and he had my back at a thousand degrees if anything popped off. After the tour he asked me if I had an idea who this person could be? Because he had a friend who could find out the problem for me, but it might take a little time. His name was Little Man, and he was a killer from hell. I knew that everything was coming to a head, and getting ready to hit the fan. Then I called Angel! She was glad to hear my voice, because I had made a safe trip to Florida. I asked if Jay was playing his role? Yes, she replied! He's doing what he needs to do to survive, and did you hear about Taz. No but why! Last night he was found out North in an alley naked. There he laid with two shots to his chest, and four finger missing. He was shot with a 357! The murder was labeled one of the biggest shooting this year. How they explained it on the news, and it was a hit. I just chuckled because I knew that Rabbit and Nut took care of the prospect. I told her to keep a close eye out on my family, because I'm going to return as soon as the shit hit the fan. Then I hung up the phone, and told them to be safe. Telvin standing there wondering if the call was good or bad. I smiled and explained to him about the Taz situation. I still could feel in my heart that someone else was tracking my every move, but one down and more to go. I asked him what was it to do in the big boot state of Florida? He said everything from fucking hoes, to going to the club popping Don P. Then he sat down, while Sunshine stood beside him with her hands on the hips peeping my every move. I knew she was his game Pitt, out for blood watching out for his safety. So I made my way outdoors to get a little fresh air, and I was greeted by another hoe. Her name was Star! She stood 5 foot 10 inches, hazel brown eyes, with a silky brown skin tone. I knew she was his number one hoe of the flock, because she stood there shitty sharp. She asked if I liked it down here in Miami? I just nodded my head yes, but I could still feel the home sick vibe running through my body. Then I heard Telvin making his way outside. He stormed outside and asked me if she was making me happy, because we were like brothers. I could feel he got Star's attention, because she grabbed my arm and took me into her bedroom. She asked what would I like her to do to make me happy? I knew it was time to shine with a sexy queen of my choice. The room started to get hot! I could feel her soft, warm, hands rubbing my shoulders to figure me out. I closed my eyes for one second, but when I open them! She was standing in my face naked, ready to get down to business. After dropping to her knees, and slowly unbuttoned my jeans it was on like a pot of neck-bones. I felt the wet warm, moist feeling of Star's tongue sucking my dick. Away she went nonstop! Still looking me dead in the eyes getting the job done professionally without a mistake. I thought to myself why was a sexy lady of this nature living as a hoe. The more I thought, the more she slurped and sucked me dry. It took my mind far from the street life, and who really wanted me dead. So I kept my mind on what was in front of me. Then my phone rang and it was Angel! She explained, it was vehicle down the street waiting for the individual to come from out your house. It was two men sitting in the blue Nova waiting on the person. I couldn't tell who they were Dee! However, from the front door came running a man out to the Nova pulling his pants up. As they drove off, I followed them out South in the projects. I stayed a little way off, so I wouldn't be spotted on their radar. I looked around the area, and I could see the car you gave Jay to drive. I quickly explained, for her to call Jay and alert him of this situation. I hung up the phone, and looked at Star while she still was handling her business. When Angel called Jay! She explained, it was a vehicle parked outside with three cats in a blue Nova waiting for someone to come out the house. She could see the lights in the house click on to see what lingered around the house. Then the door swung open, and four of Jay's boys swarmed out to peep the area. The blue Nova speeded off into the wind because they were sitting ducks with their guards down. Jay walked outside and I knew the coast was clear. She greeted Jay and told him to be safe in these streets. Then she explained, they were posted up watching the house for about thirty minutes or more. After the fact I was called! I asked if Jay was ok? I told her and Jay to watch there self, and Angel to get away from the area. Because something fishy was in the air and I couldn't put my finger on it yet. The shit is getting ready to hit the roof as I planned. Please get back to your side of town, so she would be safe and out of harm's way. Plus, she wouldn't be peeped out with my new moving dummy. She knew it wasn't Jay I was worried about it was her and Diamond. I heard Angel telling Jay it was time for her to get back to the spot, and for him to be safe. She told me what happen didn't effect Jay at all. I told her that it was a good sign, and for her to have her eyes open at all times. Then I hung up the phone! I had to stop what me and Star had going on, because I had to ask Telvin for Little Man's number? Because there some shit getting ready to go down in the Ville, and I need him to clean up the mess. He stood there in pain thinking what was next! Then he called Little Man and told him to meet us at the pimp palace. Telvin stood there staring at me with a disappointed look on his face and blurted out. When you send him out to do something, you can't turn back the hands of time P. Then he turned around to go back into the house to wait on his arrival. One hour went pass and I looked out the window there sat a white Dodge Ram in the driveway. Two cats got out wearing gators head to toe. It was Little Man and his side kick Duper! Immediately we got to business! I explained the situation, and what needed to be done. Quickly, they were in the wind, so they could catch a flight to Louisville. Away they went to seek and destroy a signed up target. I could feel all the pain lifting off my chest because everything was in motion. I asked Telvin lets go see the town? However, have fun while I'm here kicking it. He just smiled and grabbed his keys, while making his way towards the vehicle. Star was coming out of her bedroom, with a surprise look on her sexy face that caught my eye. She asked if I had a nice time? I stood there thinking to myself, should I go for round two or go kick it with a player. Then I told Telvin I needed to finish were I left off! He just laughed because I let pussy cloud a player's way of thinking. The she grabbed my hand and walked me back into her bedroom to finish round two. Then we slowly undressed, so we could get started were we left off. I laid there naked wondering that life couldn't get know better than this. She climbed into the bed, and sled in between my legs, and started kissing my thighs. Then making her way towards my champ! I could feel a soft, touch doing a circler motion around my dick that gave me the chills. After she made her way up face to face, she placed my champ inside her diamond shape wound. Star started making herself go up and down like riding a bull. I could see in her eyes love/pain that her body enjoyed. Hot sex for about three hours! Then my cellular began to ring and it was Angel! She explained the word in the streets was I had a hit over my head. I told the twins to stay away from Jay, because everything was getting ready to come to the light. I'll find out who really wants me dead! Then I hung up the phone, and thought to myself about the negative situation I just heard. Star still taking care of business like a solider nonstop. I had to stop the loveable moment, because my mind wouldn't let me focus on a queen. My mind felt like I wasn't even there, and my family was in trouble. Then there was a knock at the door! It was Telvin! He explained that Little Man and Duper just landed in the Ville. I knew everything was getting ready to go into effect. He just smiled because Star had my mind in another place focused on a dream. He turned around and walked out the door chuckling. Then blurted out, take your time young man, and I'll be in the living room watching television P. I continued to take care of her sexual needs with life itself. In the mist of taking care of my business, I just pictured my family situation. Star stopped and ask, if I was ok in a sexy voice? Yes, I'm ok sweetie! Then rolled over while sitting up on the edge of the bed covering my eyes to hide the pain. I heard her whisper my name! I just got up and grabbed my clothes hiding my true feelings. Then went into the living room to meet Telvin. He was sitting on the couch with two hoe's sucking his dick. After I was spotted the hoe's, they stop what they were doing and made their way into Star's bedroom. He got up and stood by the window, having deep thought about his own lifestyle. I got his attention and asked about Little Man's call? He explained, now were waiting on the outcome P. This negative shit that is happening with you must end today. Then turned and looked back out the window. I stood there thinking to myself, that everything is getting ready to come to a head. So I made my way outside of the pimp palace to catch a little fresh air. It felt like a new world outside! Hoe's were everywhere taking care of the yard work. One cutting the grass, while several spraying, washing, and shinning up the H-2 Hummer, getting it ready for its new adventure. I just stood there amazed, because he has come a long way in the pimping business. All I could remember is a little part of our life when we were Square Jo's. I could hear him making his way from out the palace. He explained, that he was upset about the current situation. Suddenly my phone began to ring! Angel informed me that she has been spying on Jay. He's being tailed by the same blue Nova, with light tented window and three cats in it. I could hear the fear in her voice, that's when I knew things were drawing closer and closer. So I told Angel to go home and stay posted by the television. Then she could catch the information from the news. Ok she responded, while hanging up the phone.

# CHAPTER 12

# *The Grand Adventure*

On my way towards the vehicle I looked at Telvin, but he continued to walk to the H-2 Hummer. As soon as I climbed into the vehicle, I could see in his eyes contained a painful feeling. He knew something was popping off in Louisville, and that it was a bad sign. I told him I needed a drink, so we made our way towards the sport bar in Miami. When we pulled up, it was like a king arrived! Bitches and hoe's greeted us at the door as if we had arrived at the Grammy awards. It was off the chain inside the sports bar! There were three females to every one male. I was in a daze! I was in paradise once again, and the painful news was fading into the mist. Telvin started introducing me to his friends! I felt like I was a horse running at the Kentucky Derby! My mind clicked into a zone of its own, and I knew I had to be the player I became in life. Then we made our way towards the bar for a few drinks, and Bud Ice was out the question. I ordered two shots of Crown on the rocks to get my day started. While sipping on the Crown, I could see a female making her way across the room. She was light skin, with long black hair, and a sexy ass walk. She reminded me of the twins! Then the female walked pass me and approached Telvin. They started up a conversation like they knew each other. She asked him who I was, and if I was from out of town? He just smiled and looked at me with a slight grin on his face. I knew that something slick was in the air, so I just played my roll and kept a cool attitude. I fixed my mouth to converse to a beautiful black queen. She said that she was from Atlanta! Therefore, I asked what was her name? In a sultry voice she relied! My name is Taffiney. She said her name as if she was singing softly to me personally. She began to asked questions after question. The sexy moment of her lips, and brown eyes had me in a trance. I knew without a doubt that Ms. Taffiney was a fine, educated female with a lot of class. I asked if she would like something to drink. She just blushed and said, I'd like to have a Sex on the Beach please. I ordered two rounds of Crown on the rocks for myself, after she request that type of drink. As I found myself staring at her beauty ass, all I could say was damn she is fine. I could feel my insides shacking and quivering. I was craving to lip lock with a queen standing before me, because of the kind of eye contact she was giving me. I figured she wasn't shy, but I knew it was over for me when I caught a whiff of her designer sweet honeysuckle smelling perfume. I explained, I was on a vacation and visiting a friend in Florida. Telvin just smiled, then got up and made his way to the bar to get another drink. As I continued the conversation with Taffiney, she explained she was visiting a friend as well. I couldn't help but give her my full undivided attention at this time. I politely interrupted her while she was talking, and asked if she wanted to go outside to get a breath of fresh air. She laughed and said, sure! We both stood up and went outside to the patio by the ocean breeze. It felt so peaceful outside. It gave me a peace of mind, so I could really feel what she was trying to say without any distractions. We began to understand and feel one another emotionally. I asked if she like it better in Florida or ATL. She blurted out, that ATL would always be her home town of choice. There is always something to get into at all time there. She grabbed my hand and said, so sweetie where would you rather be? I gave her the million dollar look and said, Kentucky. Because it's the home of them Country boys on the rise! Nappy Roots! She smiled as if she understood who I was talking about. I knew Taffiney was a kind of female who like to talk out her problems, and willing to work them out. I asked her if she wanted another drink. No she relied! I don't drink all the time, only on occasions. At that moment, I realized why Taffiney was in Miami! She was merely trying to get away from a problem that lingered deep within. We just stood there holding one another, like a king to his queen. Therefore, at the same time I was wondering what was next on my agenda. I could tell that she was digging my swag, but we went back into the bar to take a seat. I looked around for Telvin! I spotted him posted up in the corner pocket of the bar scoping out everything moving. I knew I was safe, so I turned to gaze back into her eyes, and it felt strange but something about her was drawing me closer. A part of me wanted to know what kind of female lingered in my presence. After I ordered me another shot of Crown, she explained she needed to make her way home to get some rest. I could see the temptation in her eyes, and the Sex on the Beach was kicking her ass. She asked if I would come spend some quality time with her tonight, because she didn't want to be home alone. Then gave me a sexy smile, I couldn't say no! I told her to hold on while I walked over to explain the situation to Telvin. Ok, P handle your business, and then we gave dap to one another. As I turned and made my way back to Taffiney, I asked if she had everything she needed? Yes, she relied! So we made our way to her vehicle, that was a 2010 Convertible Dodge Charger. The car was dipped in money green paint, trimmed in gold, sitting on some 24 inch tricked out rims. As we got into the car, I could see parts of my life changing in front of my eyes. When we arrived at her place, I knew that the negative part of me was gone in seconds. After walking into the house, I could tell that I was in a special place with Christ like pictures and portraits hanging wall to wall. I knew I was in a spiritual place full of peace and serenity. She asked if I wanted something to drink? I smiled and responded, I would like a glass of water please. As I sat there while she went to go get the drink, I wondered what was going through her fine ass mind. As she returned, to my surprise, she had a little more than water to offer me. She had on a chocolate see through negligee/teddy and I was suck, almost chocking on the water that was given to me. I was picturing how amazing she looked, and wondered to myself what was in store for me next. I began to lick my lips and smiled with a pure look of joy on my face, as if I was a kid in the candy store with 31 flavors to choose from. Suddenly there was a knock at the door! She answered the door, and in came her roommate Freda. She stood 5 foot 10 inches tall, with sandy brown long hair, hazel eyes, and thick as gumbo. Taffiney introduced me to her, and told her why I was there. I knew I had the right female, because even with that slight interruption I was still without any worries of something going down in a bad way. I felt safe! I sat there while the two voluptuous queens talked and discussed about me in detail as if I was a movie star. I laughed out loud because I knew it would get their attention, so they both could start staring at me again. After Taffiney introduced me to Freda, she grabbed my hand and pulled me in order to follow behind her. When she opened the bedroom door to enter, there were candles burning from wall to wall with a sensual aroma. I walked in the room, and it looked like I was entering a wild life safari. Her king size Bombay bed was draped with a cold black Chinchilla comforter. However, several fluffed out zebra skinned pillows, with a small size white bear skin rug laying on the floor. It was erotic that I stood back in a daze, wondering if I was going to be a sacrifice but it was going down tonight. So I laid on the soft comfortable, relaxed bed thinking to myself, it was me she wanted for lunch, and this is a small world. I would never think that she would have a side, which could make a grown man melt. Taffiney crawled into the bed like a tiger hunting down it prey, while staring into my eyes trying to hypnotize me like a king cobra. I started to wonder how I was going to approach, a female with this type of class. I knew I couldn't use the thug life method, because I just met her in the club. So I let her make the move! She grew closer and made her way to greet a king, that was waiting on his queen. Then she started to nibble on my ear, and slowly made her way to the middle of my chest. I was feeling every minute of the romantic moment we shared getting me arouse. However, my mind was still focused on what was going down in the Ville. While looking into her sexy brown eyes, I had to explain why I was visiting Florida. She looked at me like I was a stranger, because she felt like she let a stone cold killer into her home. I could understand how she felt! I was a beast rumbling through the wild life, but trying to find out who wanted me dead. I explained, I needed to get back to Telvin's, so I could take care of some unfinished business. Then she offered to take me, but I told her that I would caught a cab across town. So I could get a peace of mind while I rode to Telvin's sweetie. Then I dialed for the yellow cab to pick me up and take me to my new destination. As I hung up the phone Taffiney, in a soft, loveable voice, asked if she would see me again? Yes, I explained! I knew she was expressing her true feelings with life itself, because she reminded me of my wife. As the cab arrived, I could see the sadness lingering throughout her face, but I had to go take care of my business. So I gave her a kiss on her chick, and I explained that I had a nice time, which I would love to stay under different circumstances. Then I made my way towards the yellow cab. I open the door and climbed in, while asking the driver for a piece of paper. I wrote down my number and handed it to her, and I could see the joyful feeling jumping in an out her flesh. Away the cab went to the other side of town.

# CHAPTER 13

# *Getting Back to Business*

The ride was a peace of mind and I could still felt at peace. I pulled up at Telvin's and I could see all the hoes on guard, watching every part of the pimp palace. I made my way towards the door, then it swung open immediately. It was Star! She stood there with a slight grin on her face, because she was happy to see daddy. Then I could hear Telvin calling out my name from the living room. He was sitting on the couch, with his feet prop up on the coffee table. I asked if he had talked to Little Man or Duper? Yeah, but it some shit in the game P! Do you remember the blue Nova? The Nova was spotted over your house, and it was greeted by your wife. My heart fell to the floor, because my wife was the one who wanted me dead. I turned then walked off and went to get some fresh air outside. I felt a lot of heated flames, and I started to get light headed. Then Telvin made his way outside to check on me. He said when shit stinks, it really does stink Player. My eyes began to full up with water, because what I loved wanted me dead like a vapor, silent, quick, and deadly. I knew it was time to make a grand appearance and greet Satan face to face. I told him to book the flight to Louisville, as soon as he could. He could see in my eyes a part of me he never seen before growing up. Then I turned and walk away in a deep state of mind, thinking to myself why would she want me dead. I went into the den and stood by the fireplace, thinking how my kids would feel when the shit hit's the fan. I knew in my heart the kids needed their mother in life. Then I walked back outside and gazed at the stars thinking why did I become a drug dealer. An hour went by and then I made my way towards Star's bedroom. I knocked on the door to respect her privacy. I could hear her say come in, the door is open. She was sitting in the bed watching television, eating fired chicken, mashed potatoes, corn-on-cob, and jiffy cornbread. I walked over and sat on the edge of the bed. Star struck a conversation about life itself, and I could feel the great relief race through my body. She explained how Mathew 7 states, judge not that he be judged and it measures down to you, then smiled. I could see that she was trying to cheer me up, and see a smile appear on my face. I was loving her style because she was a game Pitt, ready to lock on and shack something to death. I laid there for an hour thinking to myself, and I felt the room getting dimmer. Then I was asleep! The next morning, I woke up by the good smelling aroma of breakfast. When I went into the kitchen, I was greeted by Telvin and three hoes. My plate was already fixed on the table, I just laughed. I took a seat then Telvin blurted out, expect the good with the bad. I knew he was right, and I would surprise someone who wanted me dead. I ate my meal, while the hoe's walked around butt naked cleaning, cooking, and getting tonight meal ready for a king. I really couldn't believe what I was seeing because today just started and the hoes were already at work. I just thought to myself, what does it take to be a pimp of that nature and laughed. I finished my plate, then asked for seconds. One female gave me another plate of food which covered the whole thing. She stood there with a gold skin tone, blue eyes, and a body like a coke bottle. I wanted to grab her, and let the champ go to work. After the meal me and Telvin went and stood on the porch watching the hoe's catch a morning breeze. There were two hoe's having a water fight, while washing the H-2 Hummer.

When they peeped Telvin on the porch, they put a little pep in their step. He asked if I wanted to go to the strip club later on tonight. So we could clear our minds before boarding the plane. Yeah that cool with me! I knew today was going down, so we went to get prepared for the club. As soon as we were dressed he told me to watch this player! Star get dressed were going to the club. So she got dressed and away went to the strip club. Then my phone began to ring and it was Angel! She explained, that Jay was dead. He was meeting a buyer, and two cars blocked him in an opened fired on the vehicles. The vehicle looked like a pack of Swiss cheese, and he was pronounced dead on sight. I knew this was to happen, running through my head. I told her I was going to book a flight tonight. Telvin sat in the back seat patiently waiting on the news. I just turned and looked at him, and told him about the Jay situation. He dropped his head, because if I would've went on my inner feelings I would be laying froze. I explained for him to call Little Man, and ask them of their location. Then see if they done got close to the source that wanted me dead. He quickly called Little Man! He explained, he watched everything from the first shot fired, until the last. Plus, the blue Nova was present on the sense. So after the gun play, the car was spotted at your house again this morning talking to your wife. I sat there looking at Telvin with a shameful expression on my face. I wondered if my wife was in on the deal, or just got caught up in the cross fire. Then I burst into a up roar! Therefore, it dawned on me, because my wife wanted to know my every move. It was to track me down to erase a Player. Telvin asked me to calm down, and focus before I explode. I could feel him at a hundred percent, but I was really pissed at the fact my wife wanted me dead. So I just overlooked what I heard on the phone, and prepared for the ladies at the club. When we arrived at the club it was off the chain, with bitches everywhere dropping it like it was hot. I was back in the right state of mind, ready to get the party stated.

As we approached the club, I ran into an old cat, I heard about by the name of Lamont. He stayed in Tennessee, and just got married. He explained, they were visiting Florida him and his wife. He told me that he owned three soul food restaurants. I explained, I was from Kentucky and I might need a job when I come back home. He just laughed because he could tell how I was dressed; I didn't need a job. I was dressed gator head to toe, and I was full of shit. When we entered the club, I made my way towards the bar for drinks. After getting the drinks we went and took a seat in the corner of the club to start a hell of a conversation. Then Telvin flagged for the waitress to come our way, so he could get change for the hoe's dancing. He asked if Lamont wanted something else to drink? He wanted a Vodka straight, while me, Telvin, and Star wanted three Crown on the rocks. It was all kinds of females running around the club that caught my eye. From white, black, and even Cuban, all out to get that mighty dollar. I could see in Telvin's eyes more hoe's that he could place on the track, if they had the right coach. I just laughed thinking that the time was growing closer to catch the booked flight. As time passed it was 8:20pm, and we had one hour forty-two minutes to get on the plane. I got Lamont's cellular phone number, and explained I had a plane to catch. I told him when I came to Tennessee, I would look up Momma's Home-Style Soul Food & Diabetic Friendly as soon as I got there. Then I turned and walked outside the club, because it was time to set it off in my home town. I knew everything that was in the dark was soon to come to the light. As we got into the H-2 Hummer a way we went towards the airport. When we got to the airport we were short on time, because everyone was boarding the plane. After boarding the plane Telvin explained, when I find out the truth, please be prepared to except it Player. Just keep your head up at all times! Them words meant a lot in my book, because it was the truth. I still felt confused but I stayed focused on what had to be done. As we took our seat, I could feel that devilish vibe running throughout my body like a run a way train. Suddenly the plane took off. I started thinking all the excited time I shared in Florida, was getting ready to end. In the air the clouds looked at peace with no worries, but in due time shit was going down. I asked the flight attendant for a cold Bud Ice, so I could calm my nerves. Telvin was sitting there relaxed with a straight face, because he knew it was a problem when the plane landed. The bell rang for everyone to take their seat, because the plane was about to land. It was time to face Satan Himself! As we unloaded the plane I knew it was time, because Little Man standing there calm, waiting on our arrival with his side kick Duper. Duper explained, he had some good news and some bad news. The good news was he knew the location of the cats who did the number on Jay. So I blurted out, what's the bad news! He let me have it! He just looked at me with a disappointed look on his face, and then turned to look at Telvin. Little Man explained it was your wife that wanted you dead all along. I didn't know what to think or do about this situation. I was placed in a world of pain and destruction without nothing to say. Then we made our way to their vehicle. Still my mind was in a trance, but away we went to the area were my wife was. I called the twins and told them to get my belongings, and I'll meet you at the spot. Then I explained for them to suit-up, because everything had come to the light.

# CHAPTER 14

# Checking Out the Spot

When we arrived at the spot, the twins were waiting on my arrival. As I got out the vehicle, I knew I was back in the game that I had to play. I could see in both their eyes a lot of pain, because of the situation that happen with Jay. It seems to them that they were gazing into the eyes of a dead man. I went into the house and sat down to relax. I explained, who I was with and why! I knew it was some hard news to lay down to a female, so I told them the situation about my wife. Angel dropped her head, while shacking it side to side. Diamond just stood there with a disappointed look on her face. Now it was time to explain the shit that was going down, because everything was on a set schedule. It was time to clean up the problem, which lingered in the streets as a drug dealer. Then Duper explained, he had some unfinished business, which he was set out to do in the beginning. Away they went like a gust of wind! I could tell that everything was going down at a hundred percent as planned. Telvin stood there in a daze, looking like he was ready to pay my wife a little visit. I could feel it was time to see her face to face. Angel left my side and came back with a change of clothes, so I could blend in with the streets. Telvin could see I was pimping in a whole new world. When she gave me the 9mm, I knew that the shit was going down like the 4th of July. I quickly got dressed so I could blend in with the streets. He stood there looking at me, because the man he saw in Florida changed in a blink of an eye. As we made our way towards the vehicles, I knew my kids would be home and I had to think fast. So away we went to my residents to greet my wife! When we pulled up, I knew the shit was about to go down now. Because there sat the blue Nova! I got out the car, and quickly made my way to the back of the house. I was greeted by my two pit-bulls! I sat there gazing into their eyes wondering how they been treated while I was gone. I could hear the twins making their way to the door to knock. When I heard the doorbell ring, I could hear Randy making her way to see who it was. Therefore, she opened it and their stood the twins. They explained, they had some money, which belonged to her husband that was stashed over their house. They could see the greed in her face, because she never took her eyes off the cash. As she mischievously thought of ways of how she was going to spend it. She stood the imaging how much money was in the bag, still standing there with fake tears rolling down her face. As they got her attention I unchained both dogs to come with me. When I entered the back door I quietly made my way to the bedroom. I could smell burning candles with the lights off. I flicked on the light, and there laid a young thug naked waiting on my wife for a good fuck. Instantly, I let the dogs loose on his ass, and ask him who's getting fucked now? The first Pit went down low for his balls, because that's the way I trained her. Woo went straight for his jugular, and he didn't know what hit him. As he screamed for help, blood was squirting and dripping everywhere. I just walked into the bathroom thinking, you no good thug scream for your life. Randy heard the loud noise and quickly made her way to the bedroom. As she ran to check out the problem! The twins stood there wondering what the hell was going on. She was in shock to see both dogs on top of a body that was almost unrecognizable covered in blood. Then to her surprise, I walked out the bathroom smoking a blunt. I asked her why? She stood there like she seeing a ghost! Randy didn't know whether to run or take what she had coming. The twins and Telvin came into the room to see what just went down. I was standing there looking at my wife out of disappointment. I asked her if this was the way it supposed to end between us. She just dropped her head, with a sad look on her face. She knew it wasn't over with and it was more in stored for her, because she had chosen her own fate at this point. Suddenly my phone began to rang, and it was Duper! He explained, that he had detained the two cats that did the number on Jay. As I clinched my teeth, I ask him to bring them to me. I looked at her while I nodded my head. I could feel positive spirits running through my body, but I had to ignore my inner feelings. So I put her bullshit far behind me for a moment, while I waited for Little Man and Duper to arrive. When they pulled up in the driveway it felt as if time had come to a standstill. Telvin and the twins went to help them with the cats they had in custody. I took another look at my wife and asked her why? Still she didn't respond or explain herself. I could feel a side of me that was confused about what just took place. Finally, the two cats were brought up close to me and I knew I wanted some answers of who wanted me dead. I reached out and grabbed the first cat by his collar, then asked him why? He just stood there with a guilty look on his face, which made me angry. I didn't get a response, so I pulled out the 9mm and let him have it with two shots to the chest. My heart felt cold! Now the other cats just laying, there with nothing to say. I turned to look at my wife and she knew what I wanted to hear but no answer. Randy was getting weak at the knees, because she seen a lot of blood been shed in her face in one day. It showed through her eyes! So I turned and looked at the other cat with a fucked up look on my face like he was next. I knew the shit wasn't over because I wanted some answers now. So I bent down beside the other cat to look him straight in the eye. I suggestively gave him an ultimatum in order for him to answer by clinching my 9mm against his forehead. He started sing like a canary and spilling the beans about everything out of fear. While seeing his own partner in crime laying there leaking without a word to say. To my surprise! He cried out that it was your wife who wanted you dead. Out of shock, I could feel the inner tears getting ready to fall from my face. My stomach balling and clinching up on me as if I was going to be sick. Instead I let this cat feel my pain, and gave him a dome shot from hell with the 9mm. Flames were racing through my veins, while staring at Randy. I gave her a look that she would never forget. We both knew the next step was going to be someone else left for dead. This was because of the conspiracy situation that just took place in the house, and one could be a problem. Randy knew she was next on the list! So she fell to her knee crying because of the bottled fear that lingered deep within. Mysteriously my phone began to ring, and it was Taffiney! I immediately told everyone to shut the fuck up, and don't say a word. She explained, that she was at the same exact club were we first met. Then asked when was I going to return to Florida for another get away trip? So she could spend more time with a king. I told her I was in the middle of handling some important business, and it was a bad time discuss our new found relationship. Plus, baby I will call you later, then I hung up the phone and got back to business. I turn to my click, and I explained, that something had to be done about this wife situation. Things were going to be off the chain, but I had to deal with now. I knew if I let her live, there were two ways out in life! Life in prison or the grave yard! So I just had to deal with the problem directly as husband and wife. I kneeled in front of her while she stood there shacking in fear. There was a sharp pain that hit the inner most of my heart. Then for the last time I asked her why? Instantly I felt uncontrollable flames race through my chest, because she was still speechless. Then out the blue she said that you know why still crying. I know you were cheating in our relationship, as she fell to the floor. I knew she was right, but to betray me was a different story. So I reached out to grab her off the floor, while telling her I was sorry. Baby a lot of these lost feelings come with the game. I looked at my partners in crime, while she faced the opposite direction. Behind her back, I gave them the signal to tie her ass up. Without her knowledge, I gently let go, and handed her to the wolves. She began screaming out of fear, but she knew she broke the golden rule. Trying to take my life! Not only as my wife, but as a member on my team period. It was too late for apologies, plus I wasn't trying to hear it! I began to make my way to the vehicle, and my mind began to wonder about a whole lot of shit. Now most of my known enemies were being dealt with in some form or fashion. I could feel a calm, peaceful feeling in the air's breeze. Then Duper carried Randy to their trunk like a pig in the blanket. As she was placed in the back, I whispered to the both of them, to follow the instructions I gave them very carefully. At that moment, I knew that Satan had a nice percentage of my soul. Telvin and the twins were standing there wondering if I was still focused on what just went down. Telvin call my name? I couldn't even respond, because I was calling a wild card call and it concerned my wife. Then I could feel Angel on one side and Diamond on the other! I felt their love revolve around my table, and everybody knew this type of shit happens for a reason.

# CHAPTER 15

## *The Hot Spot*

I hopped in the vehicle and told everyone let's go before were spotted in the area. We need to bounce now! Perhaps my wife would understand my decision, because I had no choice but to make. I sat in the car wondering about my kids, and the situation with my wife. We made our way to Diamond's house, so we could be unseen off the polices radar. As we got to the spot, I told them I had to discuss a whole new plan that had to be followed. So it would keep everyone out of the lime light! Then I explained, shit is picking up in the streets, and a lot of cats are getting curious now. Mostly about the crazy shit that happen over the last month. I know shit had been fucked up, but I have to set the streets straight. The twins standing there looking at me wondering how I felt about my wife situation. Then my phone began to ring and it was Duper. He explained, they were at the destination, where everything was to take place. I could still hear my wife's frighten screams that took place, but I had to stay strong for the click. I explain, for them to proceed as plan! He quickly hung the phone up, and made his way to the back of the trunk to get Randy. He could see in her eyes that she played the last days as a female. Then they grabbed her out, to take her to the resting place. She screamed as loud as she could, but they were deep in the country. Nothing but the sounds of the wild coyotes chained to a tree. Then they made their way back to the vehicle, so they could go back to their city. Still I continued to talk to the twins about the shit that needed to take place. They knew that I was hiding something, because of the way I was acting. Both of them knew the real reason why! I explained, I needed to take a little ride and think about my kid's situation. Then I was called with it's a rap! I could feel my heart grow cold, but still I had pain running through my body. I told them thanks for the time of business, then hung up the phone. I told Angel that I needed some fresh air to clear my mind, because it's been a stressful day. Then I turned and made my way to the car, and I could see the twins standing in the doorway. They were watching my every move as I got into the car. I sat in the vehicle wondering how does it feel Randy when the tables turn. Now wife you are the prey, without anyone to help your ass. Then I thought how I was going to raise my kids without their mother. I knew in my heart one of my kids were going to have a nervous breakdown about this situation. I could feel the inner tears, and I knew that she was still my wife to heart. So away I went to the country to speak to my wife, and ask her why. When I got to the country, it was hard to find the dark trail where the X marks the spot. After I spotted the area, I made my way towards Randy. I could hear the howling of the wild coyote's, as well as the lonely cries of my wife for help. As I approached her I asked her why? The tears racing down her face, but still she gave me no answer. I explained, if I free her would she run to the cops, and tell them everything that just went down. I was hurting inside because I was sitting there like the police interrogating a convict. Therefore, I walked behind the tree, and pulled the 9mm out then cocked it. She sat there in a frantic, because it was time to say goodbye. I shot the hand cuffs off! I explained, I loved her with all my heart, but get out of here before they return. Away she ran in fear of what just happen in her life. I knew she was going to keep her mouth shut, so I made my way back to the vehicle. Then I started my way back home, because everything was a rap. I could feel that peace of mind, and I knew the streets had a new king. Away I went back to the Ville without any worries with life itself. When I got to the city, I had a feeling that I needed to take another trip to Florida. So I gave Telvin a call, to see if he was still at the airport. He explained, he just arrived and he was ready to get home to his hoe's. I told him I forgot to tell him thank you, so I'm on my way. He just laughed out loud, because he knew something was up then I hung up the phone.

# CHAPTER 16

## *Seeking A New Life-Style*

I went to meet Telvin at the airport. When I got there I explained, I needed another get away trip so I could get my mind straight. He just laughed and went inside to get his ticket home. As he talked to the clerk he laughed out loud, because he already had two ticket just in case. I chuckled because he was reading my mind. Still as the time passed I could feel the cold chills, while sitting there thinking about my wife situation. I knew she was a silent viper on the low! As we waited on the plane, I began to explain about me uncuffing Randy and setting her free. He dropped his head then giggled, because he had already put two and two together. He could see the guilt written all over my face. Then the flight attendant ordered everyone to board the plane in a single file line. I knew that it was wrong because I didn't inform the twins of my new disappearing act. So as we boarded the plane I made my way to the assigned sit. As the plane began to start up, I could feel a part of myself running from the street life. Then I turned and looked back at Telvin. He was sitting two seats back, with his legs crossed, picking his nails, thinking about his hoe's. Then the plane took off, I knew I was going to leave a part of me behind in the Ville. When we entered the sky, I felt that peace of mind again. I knew I was keeping my promise to Taffiney, and ready to have a nice time. In the peaceful sky my eye began to close so I could get some rest. Therefore, as the hours passed we finally reached our destination, and I knew it was time to get it cracking. At the Miami airport I was still confused, because of the situation I left my wife in. So I had to block the negative thoughts because I was here to have a nice time. As I made my way through the tunnel behind Telvin, I could picture Taffiney sexy ass. Outside there sat the H-2 Hummer with two hoe's leaning against the truck. They both open the doors like we were a kings or prince. Then immediately got in the back of the truck, while taking their shirts off. I could tell Telvin was getting a kick out of it, because this is his type of lifestyle. Big Pimping! I could smell the fresh scent of baby powder, and the truck was clean to the T. He was very impressed because he smiled. Then we made our way towards the pimp palace. When we pulled up there were several hoe's lingering in the area. Hoe's were everywhere doing something with their time, just the way he trained them. After we parked hoes came running, because their pimp was finally home. He kept a smile on his face, while making his way inside the house. However, we were greeted at the door by Star. She explained, that she missed us while we took the trip to Louisville. Then she gave us both a peck on the jaw. I knew she was a one of a kind, but my heart was still set on Taffiney. I figured she wasn't expecting me back this soon. Then Star turned around and escorted me into the quest room, while helping me to get my shit situated. She explained, if I needed anything for me to give her a call and she'll be there in a flash. Then she walked away with a smile on her face. I just laughed! I began to think to myself, how was I going to live my life without the family. Then I could feel my phone vibrating in my front pocket, but my mind was stuck in a trance. As the phone was getting ready to sing its last tune, I came from out the trance but it was too late. The missed call was Taffiney, so I gave her a call back. When she answered the phone, I could tell she was happy to hear my voice. I explained, that I was back in town, and she was my type of dish on the menu. She asked if I took care of the business in Louisville? I knew she was shooting some slick questions, that I didn't want to answer. She could tell that I didn't want to hear that shit for real. So she dropped the question and explained, that she was taking a chance of talking to me while she was at work. I knew she was right, but still I was brightening up a queen day. I could understand what she really meant, so I said goodbye while hanging up the phone. My true feelings which lingered inside was trying to find a new lifestyle, with a female who lived as a Square Jo. I sat there in a zone thinking about what Taffiney said in the pass. She explained, its more to life and God is the way if you just believe. Then He'll give the world more than the body can handle. I stood there wondering if she could live in peace knowing I was a drug dealer. Still stuck in a deep thought I could hear Telvin calling out my name. He asked me if I wanted to go back to the strip club for some drinks? I explained, that I had already made plans, but I would meet up with him a little later. Then I took a seat on the couch, while he sat there focus on clips of Scarface. I could tell he was upset, because there was no response from him. I explained, about the female I meet when I was at the club we went to the last time. Plus, she's a Square Jo, but she convinced my heart that a person can change. He just laughed! Then got up and went to his bedroom to get dressed. When he got to his bedroom, Telvin blurted out love is going to get you Dee every time. I sat there thinking if Taffiney was really worth all the trouble, while slipping on a shot of Crown. I could see Star coming form out her bedroom with a smile on her face a mile long like she heard the conversation. Then she took a sit beside me, and asked me if I needed anything? She could see that I was stuck in a deep thought because I didn't answer right away. So then I turned and looked at her with a disappointed look on my face. She began explaining, if she needed to leave, and give me some time alone? I just told her that I had a lot on my mind, and I was confused at the time. I knew I was getting ready to spill my guts to one of his hoe's. So I just stopped in my tracks, and got up to go outside for some fresh air. While standing outside it was helping me to get my shit together, but I was still thinking how the twins felt. I knew these two twins could turn hell upside down, if someone got in their way. So I grabbed my phone and gave them a call. When Angel answered the phone I could tell she was pissed, because they were worried about my disappearing act. I explained, to her that I was going to take another short vacation, so I could figure out my next move. She sat there wondering what I really wanted to say. Then I could hear Diamond say ok, Angel we need to continue as plan. Everything will be running the same way you left it. After the conversation I told her about my wife situation. She just laughed, while explaining I had a guilty conscious. She was right! I had a soft spot for my wife, and they knew it needed to change. I explained, to her I felt my past was going to haunt me in the end. She knew to get the information to Diamond, because a strong empire can crumble in a matter of seconds. I told them to be safe, and give me a call if anything goes wrong. Then I made my way back inside the pimp palace. As I walked toward the bedroom, I could picture how Taffiney would feel if I went with Telvin on his club venture. I knew a female of her nature would understand, but be upset wouldn't be the word. Once I entered the bedroom, I began to get dressed for the special occasion. I knew my time was ticking, and it left me a hour from lip locking with a queen. After I was dressed, I sat on the edge of the bed wondering why I really left the Ville. Was it to close my eyes on the street life or Taffiney fine ass. Then my phone began to ring, and it was Taffiney! She explained, that she was ready to go out with a prince, and have a nice time on the town. First let's enjoy the town, and then get something to eat. Do you want to have lunch at Red

Lobster? That's ok with me sweetie! So she could destroy a pound of crab legs, dipped in garlic butter, and a side of chef salad. That sounds good and I'll pick you up in an hour tops? Then we both said our goodbye's and hung up. Therefore, I made my way into the kitchen to speak to Telvin. When I entered the kitchen he was sitting there with his legs crossed reading a newspaper. So I got his attention! I explained, that I was getting ready to go enjoy myself with a queen. So can you do me a favor? Can I drive the BMW? He stopped reading the paper, and made his way to his bedroom. However, as he return there laid the keys in his right hand. He explained, for me to be safe in the car, because the BMW was he baby. I could still feel he was upset, because I chose to go spend time with a female I just met. I grabbed the keys, while telling Telvin I would see him later at the strip club. Quickly I made my way to the garage, so I could warm up the vehicle. As I started the BMW the seats atomically leaned back, so I could get comfortable. Then I could feel the warming of the seats, and I felt like James Bond in the movie the Golden Eye. So away I went to greet a queen of my choice.

# CHAPTER 17

## *Sex in The City*

When I pulled up at Taffiney house I could feel a silent presence of peace and tranquility run through my body. She was standing in the front yard talking to some kids. It gave me several flash backs of me and my family's relationship. I started thinking about my kids, and hoping that everything was fine. As she made her way towards the vehicle, I could see the joy in her face. She started explaining, that she was ready to take a ride with a king, which God placed in her life. I just smiled, then gave her a kiss on the chick. I told her how nice she looked, then she began to blush. I could sense the fire of love racing through her body. So I quickly opened the passenger door to be a gentleman. As she got into the vehicle, I gave her another kiss and smiled. I closed the door, then made my way to the driver seat to get the day started. However, there stood two girls telling her bye. Then one blurted out, you have a nice woman sir! The shit really shocked me, because I wasn't expecting that from a young kid. I told them both thank you. And to be careful. I could feel the cold chills running through my body, like I just seen a ghost. Then I turned and look at the two girls, while throwing the thumps up. They both smiled and skipped off into the mist. It felt very strange to me, so I drove off with my queen. On our way to Red Lobster Taffiney asked me why did I return to Florida so soon? I explained, that

I had to get away from negative people, before I committed a devilish crime. I knew could feel what I meant, and I mean every word. Because I kept my promise just like I said I would. As we arrived at the restaurant she began explaining, that she was going to take a vacation to Atlanta, so she could visit her family. I want to know if you would like to join me, so you can meet my mother and father. I quickly throw a curve ball, and told her I was tied up in some business shit. If the situation gets resolved, I wouldn't mind. I had to think fast, so I hurry her into the restaurant. This shit had me thinking about the good time my wife and I shared. Now was just labeled a myth! So I grabbed the door and escorted her in! I could tell she was loving every minute of me being a gentleman. As the waitress took us to our table, I asked her how does it feel to live a regular lifestyle. She explained, it was hard, but it beats looking over her shoulder every day. I knew she was right, but that was the only lifestyle I knew how to live. I took a sit, and told the waitress could I be served now. As we ordered the food, I asked if I could have something to drink ASAP? Away she went to get the drinks! When she returned with the Bud Ice and Blue motherfucker, I was knee deep into questions. So I quickly took a drink of the cold Bud Ice! As I took another sip of the beer, I explained that I returned because I admired something about her the last time I was in town. She sat there with a sexy grin while telling me thank you, and holding tight to my hand. Still she knew I had something on my mind, but I was blocking it from the world. Minutes later I could see the waitress making her way with the food in hand. As she placed it on the table me and Taffiney said our grace, and began to attacking the crab legs full throttle. Away we ate! I knew she was enjoying herself, because garlic butter running down her mouth like sperm. I just giggled and wish it was mind! Then my phone began to ring, and it was Telvin. He explained, the club was off the chain, and it was five hoes to every male. It really did make me think, but Taffiney was enough woman for me. I told him after I get through spending this quality time with the lady of my dreams I would be there. While listening to Telvin, I sat there watching her slurping on the crab legs and chasing it down with a sip of the Blue motherfucker. I knew she was trying to get my full divided attention, and she was doing a damn good job. So I told Telvin, that I would call him back in just a minute. While eating the crabs she stared deep into my eyes like she was a zombie waiting for another meal. I knew she had deep feelings for me, because she couldn't keep her eyes off the prize. I told her that the crab legs must be her favorite dish, but go ahead and eat them before they get cold. I could see in her eyes that she wanted to ask me a personal question about my lifestyle. So I had to get ready to lock and load my heart. It was time to dodge the frighten bullets, because she had a question from hell on her tongue. She asked if my kids were fine? I knew it was time to spill the beans, and let her know of my marriage situation. So I went ahead and let her know I was married, but I was filing for a divorce. She just dropped her head, and stared at the floor with a disappointed look on her face. I knew it hurt, but she didn't let me finish the story. I quickly pulled her close and explain my wife was having affair with another man. She could tell it was hurting me to talk about this situation, but it was time for her to know the truth. Then I changed the subject and told her why I came back to Florida. I promised you I would return like a thief in the night. I feel that it something about you that has drawn me close, like I been knowing you for years. I knew I was talking from the heart. Then I asked if she was full yet, and ready to go lay down? She explained, it's still several crab legs on the plate, and I wasn't wasting a dime. I just laughed she continued eating more and more seafood. The more of the Blue motherfucker she drunk, I could see a freaky side get ready to be released. So I sat there watching her destroy the seafood, like she was at war with the world. I told her that I had to make a very important call, so I gave her the money to cover the bill. Then I walked outside so I could talk in peace. As I stood beside the BMW, I thought about a lot of shit, that needed to be dealt with in the Ville. Ten minutes later out came Taffiney rubbing her belly because she was stuffed from all the damn seafood. So I walked around the passenger side to let a queen in. As we sat there I asked her what was next on the agenda? She explained my house! Away we went to her residence, and I knew it was time for phase two. When we arrived at her house I could tell she was tired as hell, because she was dozing off on the way home. Therefore, as we made our way inside the house, I knew it was on and popping. I was going to be a honey sickle getting ready to be ate by a bear. I could feel the calm, relaxing breeze of being safe without any worries at all. She asked if I wanted something to drink, before she went to change her clothes. I explained, that I was fine but thanks anyway! She just smiled with a sexy look on her face, which could cheer up Satan Himself. Then she turned around and made me follow her into the bedroom. When I entered it was a strange vibe rush through my body. I had a feeling that I was going to be a Christian sacrifice. She had holy pictures lingering wall to wall, with burning candles in every corner. As she laid across the bed naked waiting on a king to save a queen, I knew she was ready for phase two. So I slowly got undressed, then clawed into the bed to get the game started. I sat there thinking if I should make the first move, but she was on top of her game like a tiger searching for its prey. She immediately climbed on top, and placed my champ inside her diamond shape wound. I was frilly shocked, because it felt like a Christian girl gone wild. I could feel the warm sensation of human fluids revolving around my champ. Then she began moving up and down like a seesaw. I could see her eyes rolling to the back of her head still lusting for more pain. Loveable pain that is! I knew this type of love affection was just the beginning, and it was going to be a long night of romance. I quickly rolled Taffiney on her back, and began to pull her legs towards the ceiling. Then I slid between those golden brown thighs and went to work. I let the champ do all the talking! The moans of love could wake up the dead. I felt more sweat racing down my face, because of the energy between both of us. She sat there with her eyes closed gripping on the sheets, because of the multiple orgasms which she was having back to back. So I rolled her back over and gave Taffiney a kiss. She began opening her eyes with a surprised look on her face like she never done this before. I could see she was waiting on roll two, but too much loving could set up a fatal reaction. I just laughed, while asking her to fix me something to drink. My throat was bone dry! As she grabbed the rob, I clicked on the television to see what was on the news. The news was talking about a hurricane was spotted in Ft. Lauderdale, but it was forty-five minutes away from us. When she came back into the bedroom, I told her the breaking news. She explained that we had nothing to worry about, because we were far from danger. Then I took a sip of the grape juice, and asked how did she feel about me being in her life? I could see this question caught her off guard, because of the way she looked at me. So she just smiled responding that it's your smile, and the way you treat a lady. Therefore, I explained, that I was in a relationship with a woman who didn't believe in respect. It hurt to say things about a woman that I once loved. I knew Taffiney wasn't from the streets, so I had to talk with book sense. It felt good talking to her, because I was getting to release all my pain built up inside. Still as we began to talk about my wife situation, I was thinking how I was going to keep her from my dark world. She began explaining, that sitting there holding me was making her feel like it was more to life. But inside I could feel that she was still fighting a past relationship with someone else. Then Taffiney asked when could she meet the kids? This was a question from hell, because a part of me was running from the family life. I started feeling like a dead beat dad, because I left my kids without saying goodbye. She could see the conversation was starting to frustrate me, so she changed the subject. At that moment I felt reassurance, her love meant everything to me. Still I sat there wondering how I was going to handle the wife situation. I didn't want to lead Taffiney on. She was the type of female I had searched for my whole life. But having her on by my side, and dealing with Randy was going to be a problem. As she laid there asleep, I just looked at how peaceful she looked. I began to think about the twins! I knew they were out taking care personal business of mine. As I dozed off into a deep sleep, I began to have nightmares about my wife. Being married to her was making my life complicated! The nightmares were so real, I woke up in cold sweat, but trying not to wake Taffiney up in the process. It was too late! She asked if I was ok? I almost forgot where I was at the time! We both laid back down together, while I held her as tight as I could. Not knowing what was going to happen with us, because of my wife situation. When we got up the next morning, I knew I had a lot of business to finish with the twins. Taffiney had breakfast waiting on me, and I was hungry as hell. After eating the meal, I needed a hot shower to get my day started right. Then I got dressed to leave, so I could get in contact with the twins. As I made my way to the family bathroom there stood Freda in the hallway. She was on her way to the bathroom with a change of clothes, so she could get her day started. Therefore, I stood there patiently on my turn to drain the weasel. When she came out the bathroom. There was a smile on her face a mile long, because she knew I had to piss bad. I rushed in while snatching the toilet seat up and letting loose. I almost pissed all over the toilet, because of the pressure which was being released from the weasel. After using the restroom, I turned to look into the mirror. I could see the devil trying to make it way back into my life. Then I made my way back into the bedroom, and Taffiney was sitting there smiling happy to see daddy. It felt like she was trying to hypnotize me, like a king cobra in the wild life. So I quickly laid across the bed, and she knew that she had my full divided attention. As she took her hands and rubbed my back, I could feel a strange vibe and it was on like a pot of neck bones. So I sat there thinking about my wife situation, but wishing she was the one I married first. She could tell by the way I was relaxed I was loving every minute of the back-rub. While she continued rubbing my back, Taffiney asked a million questions. Slight shit about my wife! If I was going to patch up our relationship, and a lot more of deep shit? Even to the things I was trying to erase! She was bring up my pass life, like it was time for me to be judged. I explained, that it was a hard relationship to go through, but I chose her to walk on this new journey. I could see in her eyes guilt, because she was judging a book by its cover. I knew she wasn't trying to cause a problem, but everything needed to be placed on the table right now. So I had to stop her from asking questions about my wife. I explained we had to take our time baby. I knew it surprised her, because of the disappointing look on her face. Although she started understanding that we were moving too fast, and my inner feelings were still growing. She knew that I was in my own zoon and trying to change. This was a spiritual battle between the dark side, but it was out weighting the light. So I got up like Flash Gordon, and immediately started getting my shit together. Then I explained, that I had some unfinished business to take care of in the streets. I quickly gave her a kiss, and told her I would call her later. So as we said our goodbyes, I could feel the dark part of my soul drying while the devil took over again. Once I walked out the house, I knew it was back to the street life without a doubt. I had to hide my inner feelings from her, because she wouldn't understand at this time. Therefore, as I approached the BMW I could see that she was hurt, because I didn't explain why I was leaving. Then as I started the vehicle, I turned and looked at her while blowing a kiss. Away I drove back to Telvin's wondering why I was really running from myself.

# CHAPTER 18

# *A Battle Among Myself*

When I pulled up at Telvin's, I didn't see the H-2 Hummer and I knew something wasn't right. So as I parked the vehicle hoe's came from everywhere, like roaches crawling down the walls searching for food. Bitches running with soapy rags, buckets, and a mile-long water-holes, ready to clean the pimps ride. This shit felt strange, because I wasn't use to the pimp lifestyle. After seeing the hoe's surround, the BMW like a mob, I began to make my way towards the house. As I open the door, I was greeted by Star! I asked if Telvin make his way home yet? She explained, that he was on a new mission with a hoe by the name of Jazzman. I just laughed because he was a true pimp by blood, and he was going to keep the horse stable full one way or another. Star and I made our way towards the quest room. She just stood there with a angry look on her face, like I done something wrong. As I entered the bedroom, I flicked on the light and shut the door to be alone. I started imagining what it would feel like, if I gave up my street life to live as a Square Jo. Then I immediately laid across the bed to think. It made me wonder about my old days as a normal kid that my mother raised. I could remember when my mother would disappear some night, and go kick it with some of her old friends. I knew she lived in a dark world, but kept it far from the family. This was to keep us from peeping the situation, but I was a game Pitt on game. I knew she live a split lifestyle of heaven and hell, but she was on top of it all. Then suddenly my mind clicked back into what I was really going through! I knew if Telvin wasn't home by the morning, I would have to leave a message and continue as plan. I knew he would understand why I had to take care of the business, because I was the main attraction in the streets. I just figured that he would want me to be safe, and watch my every move. I really did understand what he was trying to say, because the world was at war. Plus, a person could die in a split second in this type of game. I knew to be safe and watch everyone around, like flies on top of shit. Then there was a pleasant knock at the door, that broke my concentration. It was Star! When she entered the bedroom it felt like her present was cooling down my flames which lingered deep within. She walked over while I laid on the bed with my hands across my chest. Then I turned to gaze into her eyes to see what she had on the menu. She explained, whatever she did to upset me she was sorry. Then she turned to walk off! I told her I wasn't mad at her, because she was taking everything in the wrong way. I'm mad at myself for leaving two females to fight a war in the streets alone. The shit in the streets is driving me crazy sweetie, and something needs to be done immediately. She could feel that I was tired of running, and it was time to deal with the problem head on. She could see a part of me getting ready to play the game raw, and take matters into my own hands. The conversation was getting her weak, because she had to take a seat. I knew she was there to comfort me, but I was still fighting the dark parts of my heart. Then she changed the subject, and asked about the family situation? Quickly I explained about how much I loved my kids. However, dealing with my wife would be a problem. I felt the raging flames brewing up again, because I still could picture my wife pulling a second stunt. She could tell my wife situation was hotter than a cooking oven, because she closed her eyes. Then she told me that the hoes outside need some time management in their life, while walking away laughing out loud. I sat there with a grin on my face, and grabbed my phone to call the twins. When Angel answered the phone, I could hear in her voice a lot of pain. She explained, that it was getting hard in the streets. Therefore, everything was still running at the same pace as I left it. I could feel that she wasn't telling me something! So I told her to book me a flight back home as soon as she could, and I knew this would cheer up the twins. She knew I was coming to straighten the streets, and get down to business at a hundred percent. Then I told her to give me a call after my flight was scheduled, and we both hung up the phone. After talking to one of twins, I set there wondering what I was going to tell the streets. Still I knew I was going to display war against the people who cross me and my click. Then something made me pray! I asked God to forgive me, while I tried to fight my way to sleep? As I fell asleep, I dreamed that I was getting locked up, because of my wife situation. I could feel that inner tears run down my face, because the dream felt real as hell. I woke up in cold sweats thinking about this dream that had me worried. As I got up, I went into the bathroom to take a shower. I could feel a bad vibe running throughout my body like a ghost. I stood under the hot water, and I could feel the inner emotions going down the drain. However, as I got out the shower, So I got dressed and called Angel again! This was to see what time I was to be at the airport for the booked flight. She let me know to be at the airport at 2:30pm sharp. It was getting time for me to be headed to the airport, so I said my goodbye's. Then I hung up the phone, because I was pressed for time and I immediately called a cab. When I walked into the kitchen, there stood four hoe's in thongs. They all were wearing matching aprons cooking breakfast, but I didn't have time to eat. Star was sitting at the table like Telvin reading the newspaper. So I asked if he was back from his long night? She explained that he called, but he would be home later tonight. He wanted us to have everything ready, because we were having company. I just laughed! I knew he was working his area as a pimp. I explained, to her that she was a nice female which anyone would love, and she smiled. Minutes later, I could hear the cab honking the horn to get my attention. I could see in her face a lot of pain, because she was losing her best friend. So I quickly grabbed her hand, and I went to greet the cab driver. When I got to the cab, I turned and looked with a surprise expression. Then I told her I had a nice time, and for her to be safe. This wasn't the last time she would see me, while I open the cab door to get in. I could see her eyes starting to ball up with tears, but I couldn't waist know more time. Then she explained, that I would be missed, and I knew Star contained some deep feelings for me. Still I had shit to take care of in Louisville. So I cut the conversation short, while raising up to give her a kiss on the forehead. As the cab driver pulled off, I could see her waving goodbye to a close friend. When we arrived at the airport, I was pressed for time. So I quickly paid the cab fare, because it was 1:45pm and I had to move like the wind. Then I made my way inside the airport to purchase my ticket home. I knew it was time to zone out, and get prepared for the street life. Therefore, as I receive the ticket, I took a sit to wait on the plane. At 2:15pm sharp I could hear the sound of the flight attendant calling for everyone to board the plane. So I took my seat, and asked the flight attendant to bring me a cold Bud Ice. Away she walked off with a nice stroll, while popping her hips side to side like a model. When she returned with the drink, I could tell that she was digging my swag, because she couldn't keep her eyes off me. I handed her a twenty-dollar bill, and told her to keep the change. She just smiled, then walked towards the head of the plane to services another passenger. As the hours passed, I could hear the sounds of the alarm letting everyone know to take their seats. The plane was about to land in the Ville! I sat there in the seat with cold chills running through my body, because the time was now. Plus, it wasn't anytime to run!

# CHAPTER 19

## *Time to Heat Up the Ville*

When the plane landed everyone unloaded in a single file line. As I walked through the crowd of people there stood the twins. When I greeted them both, Diamond walked off into the mist watching everyone like a Pitt on guard. As we made our way to the vehicle Angel explained, that it was some new cats in the hood causing trouble. I could tell she was confused, but in my heart it was on like the 4th of July. She could see in my face that I was real pissed! I explained, that I was going to take care of the problem myself. As we approached both vehicles, I knew I had to rekindle the flames which lingered deep within my system. I knew it was time to get in touch with the three youngsters, and get shit in motion. Plus, I knew that they were doing slick shit behind my back, because I haven't heard from them in weeks. So I started explaining, to the twins that I would meet them at the stop in an hour. I could see in their eyes a disappointed look from hell. It was like I was going to flee into the mist like a coward, and get far away from the sense. I could feel how they felt, but it wasn't anytime to explain. I was pressed for time, and everything had to go down now. The shit had to be dealt with ASAP! I gave them both a kiss on the jaw, then told them both I was sorry. Diamond just laughed, but Angel like the devil ready to strike. Again I pulled her close while explaining, that this type of situation would never happen again. I knew that I got her attention, because her frown turned upside down in seconds. Then she smiled and gave me a hug that reminded me of Star. As they got into their vehicle Diamond sat there laughing her ass off, because it was a twin thing. I knew Angel was letting the true feelings show, but it was more than everyone else realized. We said our goodbyes, and they pulled off to go to the spot. I could see Angel looking back to make sure I got into the car safe. I knew that I needed to get some fresh air, because the shit was starting to get hot. So I drove around the city before the shit had to hit the fan. I thought to myself, if I had a chance to change my life would I do it. Then my mind went •blank! I was confused because everyone in the city thought I was dead. Now it was time to spoil everyone's dream in seconds. I drove on all sides of town wondering, which thug I was going to get first. I knew which one I hit first, it was going down like Hurricane Katrina. However, I knew the youngsters stayed strapped at all times, and they were a phone call away. As I observe all sides of town, it looked like the city was at peace, because I didn't see a drug dealer anywhere. Then I began thinking about my kids, because I seen a woman playing with her son in the yard. As I came to another stop light, I seen an old friend who played in the exact lifestyle but fell weak to drugs. I couldn't even fix my mouth to speak, so I drove on passed without saying a word. The next stop light, I sat there in a zone wondering how my family was doing at this time, but I was still stuck in a dark thought of heaven and hell. Then I could hear a loud horn from the car behind me, because I was holding up traffic. I forgot I was even at the stop light! Therefore, I drove off thinking about a whole lot of shit at once. I knew I had to make a change in life, so I gave James a call. I asked were they could be located? I could tell that he felt the negative vibe running throughout my conversation. He explained, that they were over Wayne-Head spot! So I told him that I would be over there in a few minutes, and for them not to leave. When I arrived at the house, there stood the three youngsters. They were leaning against a smurf blue Dodge Magnum on 26's banging Young Gotti, while smoking a blunt blowing time a way. As I parked the car, I had a cold chill run through my body like someone walked over my grave. I quickly got out the vehicle, and looked around because I had a strange vibe. I was truly spooked, because I felt like I was being peeped out or under surveillance. After scanning the area, it seemed to be clear so I went to the youngster with the bad news. I could see the pain written all over their faces, because it was time to put in work. I explained, that I had to make a change in life. The situation between me and wife was starting to haunt me. I felt Satan's present revolving around me in a matter of seconds, because talking about this situation was rekindling the flames. Then James blurted out, what the fuck is going on Dee? I just turned around, and looked at the sky! They could tell by my voice, that something needed to be done ASAP. Shitty and Wayne-Head just stood there surprised! Still James could see the frustration written all over my face, so he brought up a new conversation. I could feel the words which were coming from his mouth, because the truth really hurts. I was stuck in a daze, because I did want to kill my wife, but it would affect my kid's life. I looked him eye to eye, and then asked him how do you think my kids would feel without their mother?

He pulled the blunt slow, and said that would be a hard decision to make. I knew that my heart has grown cold since I've been fucking around with the click, but I still have my kids to feed. I could see the blunt was slowly taking affect over James way of thinking, because he had nothing else to say. The Kush weed smell was blowing tremendously through the wind. I began explaining, to them that I was going to take another vacation to Florida after this was done. They could tell that I had a lot of shit riding on my chest, and it needed to be cleared quick.

Then Shitty blurted out, that he understood why I needed to take another trip from the street life. Wayne-Head just ask about the supply situation? I told him that before I leave the state, I would have everything ready to go like a fast food restaurant. I explained, to the twins that they would contain the narcotic, if they needed to keep the ball rolling. Then my phone began to ring and it was Taffiney! She asked if I was going to come back, and spend some quality time with her? It has been lonely and I'm missing a country boy that was gone wild. I told her that she could get a ticket and put on standby, but I would call her when I was ready to leave. Then she explained, how much she loved me and we said our goodbyes. I turned and looked at the youngsters, and told them I had to kick rocks. I knew in my heart, that everything was going to be ran like clockwork. I told them I would call them before I boarded the plane. When I looked at James, I could see a young gangster becoming a man. I felt a good vibe about leaving them in control of my empire. Then I began to make my way towards the vehicle! As I opened the door Shitty explained, for me to be safe. Dee keep your guards up at all times! I told him that's a real statement, but please stick together like flies on shit. Shitty and Wayne-Head was cool about the situation! James stood there like he was angry about something, and he wanted to get something off his chest. They just stood there smoking the Kush blunt talking to one another. As I sat down in the vehicle, I felt good like I needed a break from the street life. I back out the driveway, then my phone rang and it was James. He explained, that he was upset about the wife situation. Dee something needs to be done about it! I understood where he was coming from at a hundred percent, but everything still revolved around my kids. Then he explained, if that was you inside the vehicle when the goons shot the car up, and left it looking like Swiss-cheese. But still the autopsy read it wasn't you, so how does this make us feel? My eyes began to ball up with water, because I couldn't respond to the question. Then he asked if I was still on the phone? It took me a few minutes to figure out what to say. I explained, to him that some things I have to let go player, or it will live to hunt me in the end. He started to understand what I was trying to say, because he had kids of his own. I knew in his heart, that he wanted to knock my wife's sock off for this situation, because she was playing the game raw. So I asked him to do me a favor? I explained, for him and the youngsters to look after my kids while I took another vacation. He paused on the phone, and took a deep breath! Then blurted out ok, because it was a family thing. I knew he was pissed off, because how could a person take care of the enemy. But he knew that my kids were innocent in this picture. I knew it wouldn't be hard to make him understand, because James had a lot of loyalty in his heart. Then I asked him to watch out for his partners, because they were two hot headed individuals. In their eyes anyone could get it in a blink of an eye. Then I started explaining, what needed to be picked up from over the twin's house. James grab 506 grams of cocaine, and split 252 grams with Shitty and Wayne-Head. So that leaves four and a baby a piece, You keep the big half yourself! Then my other line began to ring, and it was Taffiney! I explained, that I need to catch the other line, so I could get my flight date straight. He blurted out for me to call them later, and be safe while hanging up the phone. As I clicked over to talk to Taffiney, I knew she was happy to hear my voice. Because everything was set for tomorrow afternoon at 3:30pm sharp. I asked her how much was the flight? She just laughed! Then explained, the flight was already paid for by her credit card. I just smiled, but it still hurt! I told her that I could pay for my own ticket in a soft voice. She stopped me while I was voicing my opinion. She knew I wasn't use to anyone taking care of me, but your swagger contains so much street life as I can see. She had me right! I told her this is how my mother raised me sweetie. To be a man that I am. So thank you for the ticket, but let me take care of a few things while I'm in the Ville. Taffiney just laughed! It felt like she was a true physic peeping my every move. Just like a tiger waiting in the mist ready to pounce on its prey. I knew she had her mind made up, but still going to be a Square Jo for life. Then I told her I had to get ready so I wouldn't be late. Taffiney explained, she loved me and then we said our goodbyes. Away I drove to the twins house! When I pulled in the parking lot, I seen Angel looking out the window. However, Diamond opening the apartment door to greet a king of the streets. After parking the car, I sat there looking in the rearview mirror. I could see another person who was trying to find his way out the street life. As minutes passed, I could hear Diamond's hollering if I was alright? I just smiled, while getting out the vehicle. Then I started making my way towards the apartment, and there stood Diamond in a sexy fire red negligee. I thought to myself, that she was hot! She could tell that I was peeping her every move, but business came first. The closer I grew to the door, she back inside the building to stay off the radar. I could feel a part of myself getting moist, because I seen more than a partner in crime. I seen a fine female who was down to earth, but walking like a breaded model. I had to hold my tongue, because I couldn't mix business with pleasure. Plus, I couldn't let Taffiney down! When I walked inside the house I explained, that I needed to get prepared for the heat of the night. I could see in their eyes, that it was time to stand up for the things we believed in. As we walked into the living room, I could feel a piece of mind lingering in the air waiting for them to respond. Then Diamond stepped up and spoke for the both of them. She asked, if I was going to fall weak again? I knew she was referring to my wife situation, but I had nothing to say. They knew I had slight feelings for my wife, but love could get a person killed these days. I felt were she was coming from, but I had to stay focus for the home team. Then I explained, it was time for me to show my true colors, and get the streets attention. They could see the words were strictly about business! I could tell Angel understood me, because she walked towards the bathroom to change clothes. Still I stood there talking to Diamond about my wife situation, because I needed to get some shit off my chest. I explained, that I had to play a role as a father to my kids and hide the dark side of my heart. I knew my wife was down to earth, and what ever happened is in the past. Stayed in the past! I started catching feelings about the conversation, so I change the subject. Therefore, I asked who were the new cats? She explained, they were from New York, and their security was tight. Still she wanted to give them a surprise visit. I knew then it was time to show the streets who the true boss was. Seconds later, I could see Angel making her way towards us to see what the plan would be tonight. I knew I don't have to repeat myself, because she was a psycho, but ready for war. She was on fire and it was time to set a couple examples in the streets. Then I started explaining, that it was going to be a tough mission. Plus, it could be a possibility we might not make it home. Still they both stood there with a vindictive look on their faces, which gave me the chills. I hope both yawl know every minute count, and I need to make a game plan up now. I looked at the twins, hoping they believed in the things I was saying. Then I asked if they had an old change of my clothes? Both their mouths dropped to the floor, because it was on like popcorn. Angel just turned around and walked off without saying a word. I knew she was pissed about something, but away she strolled down the hallway. Still Diamond was a different breed, because she wanted to set it off right now. Minutes later, Angel came in with the change of clothes, and two armed pistols. A 9mm in the left hand, and a 223 in the other! I knew when I seen the 223, it was time to call the wild card call. Quickly she gave me the change of clothes, and the devilish vibes rumbled throughout my soul. It was on! So I made my way to the bathroom to get dressed.

When I walked into the bathroom there sat a picture above the toilet. It was a picture of an Angel reading a poem. The poem was called "The Street Life". It read! This poem is for our ways of life; To see the negative things, which revolve around the darkest parts of the street life; From murders, drug dealers, and even thugs; Trying to turn their life around, and then give the street life more love; Hoping to make way for the lost soul, which lingered into the heat of the night; Giving back to the world of pain, the respect to find the blessings of the guiding light; While understanding how God disciples tried to make a nonbeliever in the world see; To honor, respect, and have love for the world called the street life as well as me; That poem really made me think! As I looked closer into the picture, I could see the tears running down the Angels face out of pain. It made me think if I should change the plans, or do the work of Satan Himself. I couldn't let the twins down again, because the shit had to be done. So I quickly got dressed, and made my way into the living room. Then I asked who wrote the poem in the bathroom, because it caught my attention? Diamond explained, that her name was Gwendolyn. I thought to myself, that her name sound familiars. She was a snake in the grass, but the poem made so much since. She explaining, that she wrote books for a living now. I told her to get in contact with Gwendolyn, and get a signed copy of the book. Now let's get back to business, while grabbing the 9mm from off the table and cooked it.

# CHAPTER 20

# *Time to Take Care of Business*

Then I started making my way towards the door to get the night started. I told them that I would be waiting in the car, and for them not to take long. I knew Angel was getting upset, because she had deeper feelings which revolve outside the game. Seconds later, I could see them both making their way towards the vehicle in all black. As they open the door to get in, I knew it was on like popcorn on movie night. Plus, I could tell that the shit was getting ready to hit the fan at a hundred degrees. When they sat in the vehicle it was silent, and it felt like we were cold blooded killers out for negative souls. Then I asked if they were ready to take care of this situation, which was going down in the streets? Out the blue Diamond spoke up! Yeah, while Angel sat there with an unbelievable look on her face not saying a word. As I started the vehicle I could feel a dark presence hovering over my shoulder. This shit made my skin crawl! I knew right then, that it was on! It was time to judge the streets with all we had in our heart. So away we went to peep out all the hot spots in the hood. Then my phone began to rang and it was Telvin! He explained, if I needed him he was just a call away! I knew that he wanted to be involved, but it was too late. I explained, if I needed him I would immediately give him a call. Then we both hung up the phone, and I focus on what needs to be done in the streets.

When we arrived on the North Side of town, I spotted Silk. He was leaning against a black Fleetwood Cadillac, talking with two hoes like a pimp. When I got out the vehicle, he thought it was a ghost, because everyone thought I was dead. I could see by the way he was looking at me and the twins his dick was hard. Because someone in the streets was getting ready to feel the wrath of Satan. He was excited to see an old friend alive and healthy. He explained, that the streets had my name all in their mouth. So I told him to find out who the people were, so I could deal with them in my own little way. I knew he could feel all the negative energy running from my body, because the streets were giving my name a black eye. Then I turned and looked at the two female vipers! They were sitting in the vehicle with a devilish look on their faces, which could scare Satan shit-less. So I continued talking to him about the shit that happened in the streets. I knew he had the heads up on the whole situation, because he was a business man like myself. Then he pulled me to the side, while telling me who the cats were and how to locate them. I knew Silk had something up his sleeve, because he wanted me to take care of the dirty work. He explained, that he heard about someone breaking into my house, and my wife shot and killed the young thug. I sat there like I was real surprised, with a fucked up look on my face. He could see in my eyes, that the conversation about my wife was slowly pissing me off. Then I turned to looked at the twins, because it was time to get down to business. He could tell that I had everything to do with the murder of the young thug. So I explained, that the thug got what he deserved, and its best to keep their eyes open at all times in this game. He knew it had to be some shit in the game, if it popped off at my own residence. I could feel myself starting to get angry, so I asked a question that concerned the new cats in the hood? He explained, that the cats were from New York, and their boss name was X-Que. I asked where they could be found? He looked up because from out the shadows came

115

two goons and X-Que himself. I started thinking in the back of my mind, that Silk pulled a fast one on his own partner in crime. As they approached us, I could see in Silk's eyes fear like the devil was coming to judge. One goon walked on the left side, while the other one on the right! He stood there speechless without anything to say. X-Que asked him when it was a good time for them to meet? Silk stood there shacking in his boots, and I knew X-Que was going to be a problem. He blurted out a little later, with a disappointed look on his face. I could tell he was about business, because he didn't even give a fuck that I was standing there at all. Then he turned around, while blurting out don't be late. I stood there looking at Silk, because I had never seen this side of him growing up. This type of shit started to bother me, because I could smell fear in the air. I explained, this shit needs to be dealt with now. He knew that he was my way inside X-Que's door. Then I looked at the twins with a look from hell. Quickly they got out the vehicle ready to sink someone else's battle ship. As they grew closer, I picked up my phone and gave James a call! When he answered the phone, he knew it was some shit in the game. Plus, something needed to be done! I explained, that I needed back up on some bad shit now. He already knew what was going down, and asked which area? As we hung up the phone, I turned and looked at Silk. Then I blurted out this is for Jam, De'Shot, and Turtle! I could see an old spirit working its way back inside his flesh at a hundred degree. I asked him did he know were X-Que was headed? He explained, that he was headed to one of his spots, and get ready for the package to drop. I really couldn't believe Silk, because he was hiding something from me besides the X-Que situation. The I wanted to know if X-Que was his partner, because he was setting up shop in his shit! So I asked him what the hell was really going on? I need to know the business right now, because I need to know who side you were on player. He stood there like he was afraid to speak. I knew then X-Que was the boss over the North Side of town. He just dropped his head, because he felt as if I thought he was a coward. I stood there pissed, because he didn't know what was going down in the hood tonight. Out the blue he began explaining about it was a drought in the hood, and X-Que had all the work on the low. Then he said that there would be a large shipment coming to the spot tonight. I asked how much was going to be dropped off? He started shaking his head side to side with a worried look on his face. Then explained, that he didn't know, but it was going to be a lot. I stood there thinking in the back of my mind, that when everything hit the fan I might have to deal with Silk myself. I knew I didn't want to go against the grain, but he chose his own road in life as a dealer. Then my phone began to ring! I knew the call was important, so I told everyone to hold on. Please give me a second, while walking away to talk in private. Thinking it was going to be Taffiney on the phone because of the area code, but instead it was Jam. I started decoding what was going down tonight in the hood. I explained, that Silk was the door man in this situation. Then I asked what should I do about a loose link? How would you deal with this type of situation? He explained, for me to follow my heart, because the inside will not direct you on the wrong path. I knew he was right, and I had to keep faith in Silk and hope he didn't crack like glass. I asked if he wanted to talk to him before the call was up? No he explained! Just remember to follow your heart at all times. Then I turned and looked at Silk! My heart kept telling me that he would be in my corner until the bitter end. However, my conscious felt a dark vibe running throughout him. Still I was focus on what Jam said on the phone. As I continued talking to Jam, I could see the three youngster's pulling up, while peeping the area like vultures looking for the dead. I could see in his eye's the frustration. As Jam's minutes ran low, Jam explained for us to be safe. Please be safe and follow your heart at all times. Then the phone hung up! Therefore, as I walked over to greet the click, I could hear James talking to the twins. Shifty, Wayne-Head, and Silk leaning against the vehicle talking about the hood situation. I knew it was time to get the ball rolling, so I stopped everyone's conversation to let them know how everything needed to take place. Then Silk blurted out, that he had a hell of an idea. He explained, that X-Que went to get the product, and it would be easier if we wait at the spot. Plus, he would have his guards down, while everyone else lingered in the mist. Ok! It seems like a plan to me Silk, but a part of me felt lost. As I explained, for everyone to sit in the vehicles until I call the shot from hell. Then I need everybody to come in like hell was to freeze over. I knew I was taking a chance, but I had to let my click see the old me was back in town. The twins looked me up and down like it was a problem in the air. Then Angel explained, that something wasn't right about Silk's plan. I knew she was right, but the shit had to be done now. I got the youngster's attention, and told them not to let me down. I knew it was on and popping like a pot of neck-bones waiting to be severed. The youngster's standing there like terrorist ready to blow some shit up. I explained, for them to sit in the vehicle, and wait on my signal. I could tell that they were pissed off, because they wanted to be a part of the action. Away they went to the vehicle angry, because I called a wild card shot! Then I turned to look at the twins with a smile on my face like everything would be ok. They both walked over and gave me a kiss on the jaw. Quickly I explained, for them not to be late when the shit hit's the fan. I could see in both their eyes business, but Angel had a sad look on her face. She had a look on her face that gave me the chills. I told them that everything would be fine, but stay ready for my call from hell. They shook their heads, then made their way towards the vehicle to hide behind the dark tinted windows. As I stood there looking at Silk, I could tell the time was near. I asked him if he was ready to set it off like the 4<sup>th</sup> of July? He just smiled and hollered at his two hoe's. As they walked by his side him he explained, that he would call them later. They just smiled like something was going down, and I never knew I was the main attraction. Away they walked into the mist without uttering a word. I stood there with a bad feeling, but I couldn't turn back the hands of time. Plus, time waits for no man! Now down to business Silk! Where can X-Que be located? Then he turned around and pointed at Donna's building. He explained, that he went to get the package, but we will be ready when he returned. Then he asked if I was ready to get the ball rolling, and away we went towards the building? When we got to the apartment, I caught multiple chills from hell. I felt like I was being peeped out! I looked in circles to see if I was being watched, but it wasn't a soul in sight. Then we quickly made our way inside the building to get out the open. I still could feel a dark vibe lingering inside the building. The closer we grew to the door it felt like the movie "The Shinning". I pictured blood pouring from out the door like a tidal wave. I stood there thinking to myself, if I was making the right move. This was the first time I pulled a solo mission on my own. As he began opening the door, I clutched the 9mm like my life depended on it. When the door started to open, I rushed in to peep the scene! As I stormed inside the house, I was making sure Silk was playing by the rules. I hope he was keeping it real, or he was next on my list. It looked clear, so I took a seat on the couch and place my 9mm on the coffee table. I felt X-Que had his guards down, and now it was just a waiting game. I sat there wondering how everyone was thinking about me pulling this solo act. Then Silk asked if I wanted something to drink, while making his way into the kitchen? I began having multiple chills one after another like something wasn't right. Then there was a slight knock at the door! Silk quickly made his way to the door to see who it could be as he looked out the peep-hole, I could see a look on his face that made me investigate. As I stood by his side, I wondered who lingered on the other side of the door. Then he asked who is it? It was the two females, which he sent away. I knew then it wasn't right, but it was too late. I felt a heavy blow to the back of my head, that made me black out for a second. As I started coming back around there stood Silk, X-Que, and the two goons! X-Que explained, how does it feel when the shoe is on the other foot? I didn't have shit to say, while the blood rolled down my face. I knew I was in too deep, but that was just the beginning! Both goons took turns slugging me like a punching bag thirty minutes tops. In the back of my mind I thought I was going to die. Then I heard X-Que calling for them to stop, and he stood there with a mirror in his hand. When he squatted down to make me look, I didn't look the same. I look like the black version of elephant man! My head had lumps ear to ear, and my eyes were close shut. I felt like I was in a fight with Mike Tyson in his prime. I was truly hurt to heart, because my old friend change like the weather. I could feel a part of myself dying, because I had love for him. I close my eyes and prayed to the Father, because I knew this was my last ride as a dealer. Then I felt a kick to my face, that made me swallow my own words. It was Silk! He spits in my face, and blurted out you deserve everything that's coming to you with a spiteful look on his face. Then he turned around and looked at his hoe's. I laid there in my own blood with nothing to say. As he walked out the door, I knew it was time for phase two! Quickly the goons grabbed me off the floor, and taped my mouth shut so I couldn't say a word. I knew at it was time to take the long ride home! As X-Que made his way towards the door, I knew it was time for me to meet my creator. Then he explained, that he would see them after the job was done. Seconds later I was blind folded, and taken to the back of the trunk. The more I tried to get loose, the more tired I became. As I heard the trunk slam, I knew my life was on a count down. All I could picture was my click getting the news, that I was shot and killed like a wild animal. Although I could remember a song playing in the back of my head. "You only get one ride, then it's over; and it's over". I knew it was going to be my last stand with the streets, because I felt my past had come to haunt me. Away they drove towards my resting place! I could hear the goons talking to X-Que on the phone, asking him were they needed to meet after the job was done. They explained that it was going to be a clean murder, because they were going to use my own weapon. As they reached the destination, I could hear one of the goons say we are here. When I heard the doors open, I knew it was my time to die. As the trunk popped, I could hear several gun shots going off. It felt like I was in the Vietnam War! Two of X-Que's goons were hit, and one was killed immediately with a shot to his dome. The other one screamed for his life, because he finally caught the last ride. Then I was lifted from the back of the trunk, and I could hear the female's voices. I could feel it wasn't my time to die. As the blind fold was removed my eyes was full of tears, because they call their own wild card call. I knew it was time to clean up the mess! I thanked them both and looked at the goon screaming like a pussy. I just wanted to kill him on sight, but I needed some answers. I needed to know were X-Que and Silk could be found. He quickly spilled the beans! He explained, that they were going to meet over Silk's girlfriends house out North. I knew that I was going to hurt Tonya's feelings, but Silk had to die. So I turned and looked at the twins. They stood there with a negative look on their face, that could turn hell upside down. Still the young goon begged for his life! Angel walked over to me and took her bandana off, so she could wipe my bloody areas. As I dropped my head out of shame! She walked around me and hit the young thug several times in the chest with a 223. Then I asked how did they find me? Diamond explained, that youngsters were parked in the front and we were in the back of the building. But when we saw Silk walk out, we knew something wasn't right. As time passed we seen X-Que, and we knew it was a setup. Then as the apartment door swung open, while the two goons carrying you like a suitcase it was on. So as they drove off, we stayed in the mist following their vehicle to this location. Then we set it off! I couldn't do nothing but look into the sky, I just missed death by seconds. I was truly grateful because it was my time to shine. Then I asked Angel for her phone! When I called the youngster's they sound surprised, because I wasn't in the area. I told them to meet me over the twins spot immediately. So we quickly got into the vehicle, so we could meet at the spot. I was sore as hell, but I cracked a smile to let the females know I was ok. When we arrived at the spot their youngster's stood there with a surprise look on their face because I was fucked up. Quickly we made our way inside the apartment, because I didn't want to be seen. The three youngster's started going off, because I looked like I was tangling with Smoky the bear. So I explained, what really went down and Silk jump ship. I could feel Satan inside the room! The youngsters were ready to ride and handle business without a doubt. I told them Silk is mine, and they knew I had some special plan for him. Angel walked over and gave me a kiss on the jaw. She knew I needed her and Diamond to stay, because this was a personal hit. So she reached inside her holster and gave me the 2.2.3 for my own protection. I could see in her eyes, that she was willing to ride to the bitter end. I felt where she was coming from, but it was now or never. We said our goodbyes, and away we went to clean up the mess. As we got in the vehicle, I explain no nuts, no glory! I could tell that Shitty was excited, while the other two sat there quiet like a hit-man ready to kill the president.

# CHAPTER 21

# *Everything Is in Motion*

So away we went to Silk's and Tonya's resident to handle some dirty business. I knew they were conducting some type of business amongst each other when we arrived. So we quickly parked, and I knew it was going to be an easy job. Then we made our way inside Tonya's building to get shit started. Death was in the air, because it was time for someone to die. When we approached the door, I could hear X-Que talking to him about a money situation. I knew we were on time, but I felt sorry for Tonya ass. She was at the wrong place at the wrong time! Then I turned to whisper to the youngster's "no nuts, no glory". Quickly I kicked the door in, while firing one shot! The second shot was the money maker taking care of business. I hit X-Que in the shoulder with the 2.2.3, which knocked him clean over the couch. Silk tried to break for it! James gave him three leg shots, because he knew I wanted his ass myself. Tonya came running from the back room screaming for her life, but Shitty showed her know remorse. He hit her ass up like target practice! As I made my way towards Silk, I could hear X-Que being beat to death. I rolled Silk over, and he could see the pain in my eyes. He continued to say he was sorry, but sorry was no more. So I bent down and asked him how he wanted it? Fast or Slow! He knew it was time to tap out! Then I turned to look at the youngster's in action. They kicked, punched, and pistol whipped X-Ques, because he thought he was the shit. Then I saw the flash from James 45 Cot P-10 to his dome, that left him silent. As I looked back at Silk, he knew he was next on the list. So I yelled for the youngsters to wrap him up, and take him to the trunk now. Silk screamed for his life! After they got him ready, we made our way to the parked vehicle to finish the job. While they placed him in the trunk, I wondered how I did Spider over Peewee's. So I gave Peewee a call! I explained that I needed his area for a minute, and it was very important. He knew where I was coming from, so he said he would be waiting on me to arrive. So away we went towards the country to finish the job. I could tell the youngsters were upset, because one lost soul was still breathing for some reason. Quickly I explained, it wasn't over until the fat lady sing! Then all of them cracked a smile, because they knew he was going to get it. When we arrived it looked like a football field, because lights were posted everywhere. I parked and went to greet Peewee! The closer I grew to the house the door open, and there stood Peewee. He asked who was next on the meat wagon, and what happen to your face? He could see by my eyes, that it was someone close. As they grabbed the body from the trunk, I asked Peewee for some gasoline? He knew I was getting ready to give someone a dreadful death, by burning them slow. When he returned with the gas, there laid someone wrapped up like a mummy. As I slowly unwrapped the body, I could see the look on Peewee's face. He was shocked because there laid my own partner in crime bleeding. He had nothing to say, while handing over the gasoline. I poured the gas from his hips down, because I wanted him to burn slow. Silk begged for his life, but the words didn't mean shit. Everyone stood in a circle like we were at a bonfire roasting marshmallows. As I flick the bic-lighter, I could see the remorse in his eyes but it was too late. Then I pitched the lighter Silk screamed for his life, while rolling around trying to put out the raging flames. We all stood there smelling the burning of flesh, so I helped him out and poured more gas. It felt like Satan trying to rekindle the flames in hell. The more he rolled around, the more justice was being served. I was loving every minute of it! As the flames dwindled down, I could see him blacking in and out from all the pain. The I asked Peewee were his German Sheppard's? He didn't respond, because he felt that Silk had been tortured. Then I explained, he is the reason why I look like the black version of elephant man. So he just pointed towards the backyard, and I saw Nina and Eve. They look like two wolves waiting for someone to cross beyond the fence line. I could see the hell racing from both dogs like demons, and I knew it was time to show my ass. Quickly the youngster's dragged Silk to the backyard. I asked Peewee to calm down the dogs so we can get the shit started? Peewee whistled and they both sat down in the position of attention waiting on his call. He explained, for the youngsters to pitch the meat over the fence. The youngster's grabbed Silk and pitched him to the wolves. It was like pitching them an oversize doggy treat! Both dogs grabbed him quick! One struck the front, and the other grabbed the back like they were trying to rip him apart. We stood there watching the blood go everywhere! You could hear Silk crying for help, but it was going down like fright night. The more he tried to get loose, the wilder the dogs became. After ten minutes of dog war, Silk was no more. I knew the war in the streets was coming to an end. Then I turned to look at Peewee, and asked if he needed me to clean up the mess? No he explained! Then told me to go home and get some rest. I knew he seen I was tired from a long day of painful shit. So as we were beginning to leave, I felt a burst of peace in the air. I got into the vehicle, and looked into the sky. Because my old partner in crime had finally made it home. Then away we went back to the Ville! On our way I couldn't keep my mind off my kids. So I told the youngster's I need to make a quick stop before going to the spot. When I pulled up to my house, I seen Trey walking the trash can to the road. When I got out the vehicle, I could see the inner spirits jumping out his chest happy to see daddy. He ran and jumped in my arm to share the family love. Then he asked were have I been? So I quickly lied to kill the conversation! I told he I was out looking for a job to support you and the family. I knew I had to hide the pain, but I was happy to see the kids. When I entered the house Randy was sitting on the couch reading a newspaper. When she saw me I knew she got weak at the knee, because I was the last one she would expect to come home. I asked her how she was doing? She didn't even respond! Then she got up to walk away in pain. I knew she was still upset with me, because I put her in a negative situation. I explained, to the youngster's that I would call them later because I need to talk to my wife. James sat there with an angry look on his face, like he didn't approve of my situation. I told them I would be ok, then I call the twin to let them know where I was at. So away they drove in the mist, while me and my son went back into the house.

# CHAPTER 22

# *Home Sweet Home*

As we came inside the house my wife was sitting in the living room looking at the news drinking a cup of coffee. On the 11 0'clock news they showed a home invasion out North, but they couldn't identify the bodies. So she asked why was I there? I explained, that we still had kids to raise. I could tell that she was crying on the inside, but she was tough as steel. She began asking questions about my face? I told her that I got mugged, while getting off the plane by three Africans. She just laughed, because I was full of shit. As she grew deeper into the conversation, I began to let my guards down on a silent viper. Therefore, as time passed, we began to get sleepy. So I asked her if she wanted to get a little shut-eye? She just smiled, while thinking about all the good times we shared together as husband and wife. Then we made our way towards the bedroom, and I could tell her pussy was beating through the tight jeans she had on. When we entered the room, we both slowly undressed to climb in the bed. I laid there staring into her eyes, while explaining that I was sorry about the past. She placed her finger on my lips to make me hush! Then went under the covers, and place my champ into her mouth. I could feel the warm saliva rotating around the tip of the head, like she was trying to unscrew a top. As I peep under the cover, she was looking me dead in the eyes like a pro. Minutes later, she slowly worked her way to my meatballs. Licking them side to side, I guess to get my full undivided attention. My champ got hard enough to explode. I quickly grabbed my wife, and laid her on the back so I could gain control. Then I cocked her legs towards the ceiling, while placing my champ inside the diamond shape womb. I could feel that pussy jumping for joy! The warm com splashing against my meatballs began to wet the bed, and I knew she was having the time of her life. When I turned her over to hit it from the back, I knew I was going to give it all I had. Randy turned around looking at me, and screamed give me all you got daddy. My eyes lit up like a Christmas tree, and my champ almost exploded like a fire cracker. As she turned forward, I knew it was on! I began to ease my champ inside her womb slowly, so she could feel the full effect. I gripped both ass chicks to gain control, and away I went full throttle. I bang the pussy like it wasn't no tomorrow, to let her know where I was coming from. I could tell she couldn't take it, because she laid on her stomach with her face smothered into the pillows. This was to calm down the moaning, and it wouldn't be so loud. I could feel the bed becoming a swimming pool, because she couldn't stop cumin. I could hear Randy saying she loved me, but I was still cooking the chicken. After the long romance I could see my wife had enough, because she laid there shaking from the multiple orgasms. Still I was tired as hell, so I grabbed my wife and curled under her to get some rest. As she rubbed my head like a doll, I could feel my eye closing fast. Minutes later I was out like a light! So as time passed, I was woken up by the smell of breakfast and three metro police officers. I thought I was still dreaming, but the shit was real! One officer started reading me my rights, and I knew then my wife put some shit in the game. The other two officers explained, I was being arrested for the kidnapping of my wife. I tried to plead my case, but they didn't want to hear a word. Then they told me to get dressed! When I finish getting dressed, one officer placed the cuffs on tight. I knew that everything was coming to an end, but only God could judge me in this situation. They explained, that my wife was willing to testify on the witness stand about what happen to her. As the officers escorted me out the house. There stood my wife with a negative look on her face, that slick pissed me off. I asked her why? She explained, You, know the reason why! Then went back inside the house, and slamming the door. My heart just dropped, because I could feel my inner emotions from last night's romance. So now I know my wife just played me like a fiddle! As they escorted me to the Swat vehicle, I could see my neighbors looking surprised like they were locking up a celebrity. When they placed me inside the vehicle, I looked back and I could see my wife pecking out the blind. I just lean back for the ride, and could tell my luck was truly running out. Then away they took me to jail to be booked for kidnapping.

# CHAPTER 23

## *The Clink*

When we arrived, I felt I was getting ready to be placed on trial for some more shit, because the news cast was waiting on my arrival. As I got out of the vehicle, cameras were everywhere in the area. Reporter's yelling out several question, but I didn't answer! I felt that I was being setup for a murder case. Quickly the officers escorted me inside the jail, so I could greet the commissioner. When I approached him, I knew he had my life in his hand. He stood there reading out my charges, with a frown on his face. I tried to get his attention, but he had nothing to say. After reading the charges, he explained my bond was set at a quarter million. Then told the officers to get me out of his eye-sight. I knew then it was really over! As the officers placed me inside the four corner caged in cell, all I could think about was James in the back seat. He looked at me like this isn't right! I knew I should have listened, but I let my inner feelings get in the way. Then I started thinking about what my wife's intentions were, but I knew they were far from being good. I should have known not to let my guards down on a snake, because it only takes one slip and you are out. So now I know I have to accept my punishment like a man. Then I called for the officer! As I got his attention, I asked if I could get my one free call? When he opened the cell he explained, for me to make it quick. So immediately I grabbed the phone, and called Angel. When she answered, I could tell she was waiting on my call. She explained, I was all over the news like a serial killer. Then she asked if I was alright? I explained my situation, and let her know of my bond. Then there was a moment of silence on the line, and I could tell it was hurting Angel to heart. I let her know my wife had me arrested for the kidnapping, and taking her to the country. Angel knew I was facing some hard time, but something needed to be done ASAP. Then I could hear the officer telling me to say my goodbye. I told her to be safe, and call my attorney. Please explain to him my situation the best way you know how sweetie, because I have to go back in the cell. Then the officer clicked the power, and I really didn't get to say goodbye. So I gave the officer a nasty look from hell, while walking back into the four cornered room like a slave. As I took a seat on the cold hard bench, I started thinking about Taffiney. I knew that it would hurt her to know I was locked up, but I didn't want to keep her in the blind anymore. Especially, if I was ready to kick out a relationship. As the day passed I grew hungry as hell! The officer came and brought me a brown sack lunch. The sack contained two bologna sandwiches, chips, and a juice pack. This shit made me pick through the food, because I felt like I was starving Marvin. The bologna was cold, old, and had a green tint. Therefore, the shit was starting to freak me out, because I wasn't use to the jail lifestyle. So I had to fight my way to sleep, because I couldn't believe what my wife just did to me. After I fell asleep I began having a freaky dream about my wife that had me mad. Then I was awakened by the sounds of an officer hollering out chow time. I could see inmates lining up in a single file line waiting for their tray of food. I didn't know what to do, so I just followed suite. As I got my tray I went to take my seat, and I could hear my lawyers voice. So I gave my tray away, and went to the door to wait on the officer to call my name. When the officer open the cell there stood my lawyer dressed in a silk black suit, gators, clean to the T". I began explaining to him about my wife situation. Then he told me that there is some good news and some bad news. The good news is that your wife doesn't want to testify, but the bad news is if they let you go without being punish she will testify. She will sing like a yellow canary bird ready to spread it wings. Then he explained the judge was willing to sentence you to 12 years at 30 percent in prison with the eligibility of parole. I thought to myself that it was about 48 months to kill the 12 years, but 4 years wasn't long at all. Then he told me to keep my head up, and I knew it was time to step it up. He explained, that he would have it on the docket in a day or two. I just smiled to let him know I was willing to take the charge, and go ahead to prison to do the time. So away he went to get the job done, while I walked back to my cell. When I walked in my cell my lawyer stopped me in my tracks, and told me to stay strong. Now I had to find a way to sleep these days away. I knew that this was going to be a hard task, but it had to be done. I stood there like I was in a daze, because my days as a hustler was coming to an end right before my eyes. So I walked over to take a seat, and wait on the lawyer to do his job. When I found a place to sit, there laid a man under the bench getting some rest. As I sat there I closed my eyes, so I could fight my way to sleep to end the long day. In thirty minutes' tops I could feel myself dozing off, and I heard the man under the bench move. Then I quickly got up, so it would be easy for him to get up. I could feel a cold chill running through my body, because all the other inmates got silent. I knew then we were all surrounded by a true killer from hell. Then he asked me my name? I told him my name, and took a seat on the bench. When he started explaining who he was, I looked around and everybody else was facing the other way. I asked Donut what should I do about a kidnapping case? He just looked up, and said it is between you and God. I knew he was right! Still I sat there thinking where I knew the name Donut, and it dawned on me. Then I asked if they called him the Old Man? He just smiled, then sat beside me like I said the password. I could tell I had his full undivided attention, because of the gloss peak in his eyes sparkled like diamonds. He explained, every case contains a loop hole, but it takes time to find it. I knew he was putting me up on game, so I could fight my case without a doubt. This could help me keep my head up, while I dodge the frighten bullets of the judge and wife. Then I could hear the officer calling out my name! As I made my way towards the door he explained that I had a visit. I thought to myself who could it be! So I quickly made my way to the visiting area, and there sat the twins behind a huge glass waiting for me to speak. They both sat there with a sad look on their face, because I was locked down like a slave. So I smiled, because I could bring laughter inside the dark room. Once they seen me smile, I could tell it washed off some of the burning pain that lingered in them both. I asked how everyone was doing? They explained, that James was in the car, but Shitty and Wayne-Head were losing their mind. So we tried to talk to them both! They started talking about killing your wife, because she went against the grain for the second time. Then James spoke up! He explained, for them to wait on your call, but they stormed out the door with nothing to say. James just stood there in shock, because they were out of control. Then he went and took a seat on the couch, while dropping his head out of disappointment. I told them to be safe, because these two were hot-heads. I knew James was waiting on the wild call, so he could go handle the business ASAP. Everyone knew that these two youngster's had to be stopped without a doubt. So I explained, for them to track them down before it was too late, because I didn't want to kill someone I loved. They could tell I still love my wife, and I was going to protect her until the bitter end. The fire grew in the twin's eyes, because these two youngster's had to be stopped one way or the other. I knew it was going to be a showdown, because Shitty and Wayne-Head was on some vengeful shit. I sat there thinking how James was feeling, and if the youngsters didn't listen how would he respond. I wanted to know if he would turn on the twins, or handle the business which was placed on the table. I had a bad feeling that someone I loved was bound to get hurt. So I began to pray to God to step in, and stop the youngster's from trying to kill my wife. I could feel the multiple chills run through my body, but with an evil vibe. I knew that Satan was winning the game, and someone was bound to get killed. When the visit was over, I had to make my way back to the cold cell. As I laid on the bench, I tossed and turned to fight my way to sleep because I had a lot on my mind. After the long hours of deep thoughts, I made it to sleep! As the time passed I was awakened by Donut! He explained, that I had court this morning, and I stood there amazed because the day was now. I knew my lawyer was on top of the situation, so I got dressed and waited for my name to be called. I stood there nervous as hell, but still focused on what needed to be said to the judge. My heart rate picked up at a hundred degree! Then I felt Donut place his hand on my shoulder. He explained, it would be a cake walk if you keep faith in God. I could feel a burst of fresh air linger in the room, and I knew God sent his angels to watch over me. Minutes later I could see two officers approaching the cell! I knew it was time to go face the judge, and get the punishment from the D.A. As the door swung open, I placed my hands forward so the officer could place the hand cuff on. After I was cuff, away we went towards the courtroom. When we entered the courtroom cameras were lingering wall to wall. I got dizzy as hell, because reporters were everywhere. As I spotted my lawyer, he signaled the officers to bring me to him. I could see a slight glare in his eyes, like he just pulled off a flea-flicker. As I took my seat the lawyer whispered in my ear, if 6 years at 30 percent was enough time. I just smiled because he was working his magic! As the judge took the stand, he stared me up and down to let me know he had full control of this situation. Then he explained, I was being charged with kidnapping my wife, but the D.A. offered me 6 years at 30 percent. Quickly my lawyer stepped up and said I agree! I kept a straight face, while saying yes Sir. Then the judge handed me my papers to sign, so I could get the ball rolling. After signing the papers, the two officers escorted me back to the cold dark cell. I could picture how my wife truly felt about this situation. I knew she got the news, and she was going to hit the roof because this wasn't enough time. As I went into the cell there sat Donut reading a newspaper with is legs crossed. Once the officers began opening the cold dark cell, Donut started folding up the newspaper waiting on the outcome. When I cracked a smile, he knew the case went in my favor. I explained I had 6 years at 30 percent. He knew I just got away with murder, but God was in my corner every step of the way. He asked if my wife was present in the courtroom? I explained no, but when she gets the news she was going to be pissed. So away we talked about a serious conversation, because I needed to know about prison. The shit was starting to freak me out by the second, but everything had to sink in now. Then I asked him about his situation? He stood there with his head held low, and said it is up to God now. I could tell that he was hiding something, but trying to keep it from himself. I knew if he wanted me to know about his situation he would have told me, but know answer. So I left the shit alone, and talked about a different situation. I asked him when did the blue bus usually make its runs to prison? Then he knew I was ready to go do my time! He explained, that the bus came every Thursday, and I sat there thinking that I was the first thing smoking. Because I was one step from being free. I knew going to prison would slow down the streets business, but I had time to do as a man. As I looked at Donut, he turned around with a disappointed look on his face, like someone just walked over his grave. I asked if he was ok, but he didn't respond? I could see the pain run through him, but it wasn't anything I could do about the situation. So I felt that he just needed sometime alone, so he could get his morals together and snap out of it. Therefore, I went to take a seat, while wondering if the twins and James were ok. I knew they were on Shitty and Wayne-Heads trail, because they needed to be stopped immediately. I knew my click were true gangsters, but I just wanted them to be safe. Then I fell into a deep thought thinking about how I was going to explain this shit to Taffiney. I could feel a lot of pain rumble through my chest, because I knew if she found out about these 6 years she would be sick. It would tear her Square Jo ass apart in seconds, but she still needed to know without a doubt. I just didn't want her to have a nervous breakdown in the process. So I just laid there thinking to myself, asking God to be my mouth in action. Laying there in deep thought I slowly fell asleep.

# CHAPTER 24

## *Rise and Shine*

The next day I woke up with a peace of mind, because I felt God heard my cry. I knew He had worked out a miracle, because the whole cell was a peace even Donut. As I walked over to greet him, I could see him sitting there in a different state-of-mind. He explained that he was sorry about yesterday, because he heard some disappointed news about his own case. They offered him life with the eligibility for parole. I could tell that it was still bothering him inside, but he was a strong man to heart. I knew he could handle this situation without a doubt, but life would frighten any man. He explained, that we would ride the blue bus together and burst out laughing. Then I knew he had two sides to life, like Hackle & Jackal but covering up the pain well. I knew it was going to be a long Monday, so I told him that everything would be fine. Everything happens for a reason old school, and I smiled. I could see that stress all over his face, and I had to find a conversation to change the situation. As we talked the day away, I knew Tuesday was going to be hell on me, because I was leaving people I loved behind. Plus, I still haven't talk to Taffiney yet! I knew she needed to know that I was going to do a little time in prison for a foolish act of pain and destruction. I felt in my heart that she wouldn't understand, because I was hiding my true lifestyle from her the whole time. Still a part of me wanted to be completely honest with a female of my choice. She had a glow about herself that took my heart by surprise, and it was time to spill the beans. So I sat there thinking of all kinds of shit to tell her, but I wasn't going to lie anymore. I could feel my heart getting moist, because I had true feelings for a woman I just met in Florida. Then Donut asked if I was alright? He could tell that I was stuck in a deep thought, because I got silent as hell. I explain, that I needed to be alone for a few minutes, and figure how I'm going to tell someone I love that I was headed to prison. Then I walked over to a spot by myself, and close my eyes to hide the pain. The deep thought kicked in like a flash, and I fell asleep. The next morning, I knew it was time to hit the long dark road of repent. I felt today was going down like the wild-wild-west, because four officers approached the cold cell, and started calling out names. Donut was first on the list! Everything got silent inside the cell in a matter of seconds. Three officers stepped forward, while one shackled him head to toe. Therefore, the other two stood there watching his every move, because he was labeled a high risk. I could see the fear that lingered in all four officer's eyes, because his past history. After cuffing him they escorted him towards the blue bus to keep him away from everyone else. When they returned to the cold cell, I knew I was next on the list. As the officers called everyone else's name, we lined up in a single file line, like kids in school waiting to be cuffed. After being cuffed we were all escorted to the blue bus, so we could catch our ride. When I stepped on the bus, I spotted two of my old buddies from the streets J.D and Chris. They explain that the streets had finally caught up with them both in the long run. I knew that they were partners in crime until the bitter end. Chris began explaining what happen, while J.D sat there like a cold blooded killer from hell with nothing to say. When he asked me if I remembered Jamie from high school I nodded yes? He told me him and J.D were playing dominos for five-grand a game, and Jamie got caught cheating hiding dominos. J.D drew down on him without thinking, and gave him a dome call that left his ass speechless. So I couldn't resist and hit his partners up, like the movie Gun Smoke. Everybody else broke and ran for their life just like bitches in heat. So we began to shoot at everything in the area, while reaching down to grab the cash. Then we left the spot without a doubt, and got back to business like nothing ever happen. I stood there shacking my head, because two of my friends got jammed up in some crazy shit. I could hear the officer telling me to take a seat, so I told them I would talk to them when we got to prison. As I grew closer to the back of the bus, there sat Donut chained to the seat like a serial killer Jeffery Dommer. So I took a seat right across from him, and got comfortable for the long dark ride. As the bus started up, I felt a part of me getting home sick already, because I didn't get to explain this shit to Taffiney. Quickly I closed my eyes and prayed to God for a little understanding. I could feel a burst of fresh air hover over my head, and I knew He was answering my prayer. It just made me smile! The more I thought about the streets, the calmer I became. Then I began to doze off! I dreamed that I forgot I was going to prison just that quick. In the dream my wife was pregnant, and it was another boy. I was going to name him Carlos! Then as the dream started to get good it was interrupted, because the officer was hollering out that we were home. When I opened my eyes the prison looked like a castle on top of the hill. The officers lingering tower to tower, with their hand locked on the trigger and eye-balls on the scopes. They stood there silent watching every move an inmate made, like they were ready to blow anyone's ass off. As we unloaded from the bus, I could feel myself getting ready to enter the new world. When I walked inside the prison, it was officers standing everywhere. As we were getting unchained, one of the officers asked what size did I wear? While the other one explain for me to get into the shower, and be hosed down like an animal. After being hosed down like a dog, we were handed a pair of pants, shirt, and shoes to blend in like the rest of the inmates. I started to get home sick, but it was too late to cry over spoiled milk. Minutes later, officers began calling out several names! Again Donut was called first! They quickly escorted him to the hole, because they knew he was going to be a problem. When I heard my name my heart dropped, because this was my first rodeo in prison. As I followed the officer he explained, it was best to do my own time. I knew what he was trying to say, but I didn't have shit to say. When we got to the unit, I could see gang members everywhere. Crips on one side, while the Blood's on the other! I could feel the inner chills, but I wasn't taking no shit today. So I kept my composure, and went to my assigned bunk. When I reached the bunk there stood several Muslims reading the Holy Koran. I could tell that they were real respectable people, so I walked around to put my thing up. I could see they were in the Koran deep! They could tell this was my first time in prison, and I didn't know the ropes. So Jammel X began to share knowledge, while I made up the bunk. I could tell that he had his shit together by the way he talked, because several of the Crip's and Blood's gathered up to listen. He explained, about our ways of life, and we needed to take a stand against the enemy. He continued telling us that the devil was a lie, and the serpent placed a dark veil over all our eyes. We need to find the true meaning in life itself! The more he talked, it made me want to change my life around for my kids. After an hour passed several inmates were getting the picture, and went towards their bunks thinking about the situation. So I laid in my bunk listening to what he had to say, because the knowledge was real. After the long speech the rest of the inmates walked off to go share his message. I could tell that everyone received the message, but it was knocking out my butterflies. As I laid on the bunk he got on his knee, then prayed to Allah and gave Him thanks. After he got though praying, I leaned over to thank him again for the speech, because he took a lot of stress off my chest. He explain, no problem my brother, and keep the faith in your heart. Then I told him I was going to get me a little rest, and think of my next move in life. As I laid there I couldn't get Taffiney off my mind, but I knew she was ok. All I could picture was us running on the beach, like life guard off Bay Watch trying to save the world. This peaceful thought made my body relax, and then I fell asleep without any worries at all.

The End

# DEDICATION OF "<u>EXITING THE GAME</u>"

First and foremost, I give God thanks for the ability to expand my mind to show His children we all can change. I knew it would be hard to change my life around, but with God all things are possible and it is the way into the Light of Success. I've walked many days in the mist of darkness, but He sent Angels down to guide me along my sinful way in life itself. So thank you Carol Dickerson-Watkins, Larrika Bishop, Marie Dickerson, James Dickerson, and Carl Williams for your loving support. Without this love I couldn't reach this goal, which God placed in my path. So I hope all my sisters and brothers take the dark veil off the naked eye to see what God has planned in our life as Sinners to become Saints. I dedicate this first book of "Exiting The Game" to this world of life, and all the love ones were lost in Satan's dark world of pain and destruction.... Amen

This fiction novel has been written by Donald Beach Howard Jr. "Exiting The Game" was based on the streets activities of life, which revolves around the world today.

Thank You and please give the Lord a try......

Contact:
donaldbhoward@gmail.com

Printed in the United States
By Bookmasters